Conventional Wisdom

BOOKS BY JOHN BART GERALD

A Thousand Thousand Mornings
Conventional Wisdom

John Bart Gerald

Conventional Wisdom

FARRAR, STRAUS & GIROUX

New York

Copyright © 1970, 1971, 1972 by John Bart Gerald
All rights reserved
Library of Congress catalog card number: 74-186097
ISBN: 0-374-12892-8
First printing, 1972
Printed in the United States of America
Published simultaneously in Canada
by Doubleday Canada Ltd., Toronto
Designed by Dorris Huth

The "Song of Amergin," quoted on pages 100-1,
is from *The White Goddess*, copyright © 1948
by Robert Graves,
and used with the permission of the publishers,
Farrar, Straus and Giroux, Inc.

Contents

ONE

Memories of a Marriage

We stand there in the kitchen looking at each other and not knowing what to do. Our presents are piled on the kitchen table. Since she didn't throw her bouquet she puts it in a jar of water. She brews a pot of coffee.

We stand in the kitchen looking at each other until we realize we are going to make love. For an instant I'm sad since it is such an ordinary thing to do just after we are married, but her smile is very happy. I take the coffee off. She takes off her green dress and hangs it over the chair back. Then she takes off the rest of her clothes and stretches out with the afternoon sun on her, on our red and orange bedspread. Red, and her body is pale cream and fruits and young animal while her strong black hair flowing down her neck, between her thighs, is fact, and it says here I am, I'm

3

waiting, there's no rush for the rest of our lives, there's just us.

With her on the bed, my eyes shut by her body, I remember her looking at me on the altar, and stop and get up and go into the kitchen where her bouquet is all sorts of different white and yellow flowers. I unwind the bands of wire that hold them together and unwind the white paper around their stems, setting them free, and as she looks up at me lazy, I spread the flowers over her thighs and breasts, a flower around her neck, some in her hair like she is lying in a field back home, because I know she likes flowers, and then I lie down and we crush the flowers with our bodies. I blow white and yellow petals off her breasts, scattered in her hair, flowers in the palms of my hands promising how good it will be now that we are married, better, and we will never be alone or anxious, amid all those bruised flowers.

It is hard to get all of me under the covers without anything left out in the cold. Dark and warmer. Chin on her hip, I kiss her narrow waist, my breath burns back. Her hand touches my head, smooths my hair. Her voice is faraway icicles falling in an empty room. —Not tonight.

4

She does not mean no. Her legs are warm, her feet are cold. I touch her. She moves like a breeze and is gone. With eyes open or shut in the blackness I can see all of her stretched out beside me. Her waist is red and her inner thighs, and the hollows of her neck are red and orange, and her breasts pale white rising like mountains and her stomach is white and the tops of her legs are brilliant white, forbidding, but her hollows are red and warm. I am searching for reward. My hands are covered with sweet oil.

She lies without struggle and fights me bitterly, passive. The bones of her hips are sharp, her stomach hides under her ribs. In the dark she is cold white and only her breasts and hips are rose. I come up alongside her like a dolphin. I put my fingers in her flaming hair and play.

She lies facing up into the night. I wonder what she's thinking. I touch her eyes, they are open and dry. Her face is cool, her lips shut, her neck smooth white—she makes a sound like a pigeon and then there is nothing, silence again and the clock ticking.

—I'm very tired, I'm sorry.

—You're lying. Listening to our breaths.

She holds my hand. —I don't know you anymore. We're strangers.

—You're my wife.

She laughs. But to me she glows warm red flicker-

5

ing to oranges and rises from herself shining white like a pigeon in a nest of flames. I think her breasts will taste of cherry soda. I bind her in my arms. She burns along me. She struggles to free her arms and gives up. Wanting her will pass, if I only hold her against me and don't move, and think of what she wants. Her body trembles.

Her arms caught against my chest, she moves about with sounds like pigeons strutting in the park saying little no's. I let her go. She pushes against my shoulders. I've shed my skin and I'm alive. She's alive sighing with regret and the pigeons coo and begin to scatter, her arms helpless, her hips sharp, her ribs hard against my ribs, her breasts soft as fresh bread, her whiteness burns with a slow fire. She draws me forward, escapes and pushes me away. I want to say it's all right, things never happen the way we want. I taste her lips, breasts, and wait for a breeze through the heat. Her sounds make no words. Her hands flutter on my neck, down my back turning on themselves, she tosses upset, not smiling, her legs twist like vines, her breasts are bunches of sweet grapes, and over my hand her waist is burning, her thighs are burning, cool, moving.

I call to her silently, pleading with her to give over. I tell myself be gentle, she is very fragile, and I cradle her, losing slowly to what I want as she moves anguished on her bed of thorns until her arms come slowly around my back and deep in her throat she calls to me. I plow the coals of our hearth. The night bursts into sheets of flame around us and our bodies are burning away to free us. I search for her closer in my arms, afraid to crush her, I see her many ways at once, open to me, holding me while she talks to a stranger. Her head nods back and forth on the pillow but I know there is no smile on her lips. Her legs are canted like the wings of a bird in flight, trembling washed in a waterfall. Back in the hills I cry to her, call for her, but I can't find her. She catches my hand, her fingers slip through mine. For an instant we glimpse each other, parting, and I'm still silently begging her to smile.

She pushes the door open, carrying groceries like an armful of children. The snow is melting off her boots. —Hello, Will. She puts down the bag and hugs me. Her coat is wet.

It is new-chili night and the beans have been soaking all day in water, emitting a sour gas. A rust-red kidney bean. She cooks up several pounds at once in a large stone pot since they swell with soaking. If she doesn't soak them for a long time they soak in my

7

stomach. It's the same with white beans and most dried peas. She mixes in onions, peppers, disturbingly colored tomato paste, then bits of pre-cooked hamburger. She adds her special spices though once she forgot and I couldn't tell the difference.

If she starts with three pounds of beans and a half pound of hamburger, this with an equal quantity of cracked rice lasts a week of suppers. Toward the end of the week the chili begins to harden in the refrigerator, but then she slices it and fries. Or puts it in a sandwich. Or cuts parsley on top and hides it under carrots and margarine. If the chili gets too hard she chips off several servings and adds cream for chipped beans. Another week she'll prepare the beans a different way. Boiled beans are good mashed into a paste and wrapped in cabbage leaves. Bean salad is good in summer. And some people like beans in molasses. I buy the beans in twenty-pound bags. She buys the cracked rice at pet stores. It is a great joy to reach the end of a bean bag and start on a different kind of bean. For the white bean can be served in as many ways as the kidney bean. Pea beans are less substantial and go well in soups. Still, there is one inescapable—

She goes through the motions. At least the beans she cooks are fresh. But I am not very hungry until I imagine rare steak, baked potatoes, and two fresh tomatoes.

Finally the rice, steaming, one stubby little grain sticking to another with a square of margarine pooling in the middle. Then two large spoonfuls of chili sticking to the spoon until she shakes and lubricated by tomato paste the goods fall on the rice. The fragrance reminds my nose, the same old animal reaction, my mouth waters. I imagine running the tip of my tongue over the firm beans, nibbling one at a time between my lips, a spiced touch in a tongue of pepper, the quick bite of the onion, searching deeper for those little bits of hamburger and the frantic heat of a peppercorn. But with the first taste I am left to chew thoughtfully on what, in fact, needs no chewing.

When we are through I look up at her. —Not bad. I know she has gone to a lot of trouble to make it nice.

—Thanks a heap.

—We've changed. You won't look in my eyes. It was different. We forget. Everything worked for us, the whole city ran on our time. Put on our coats, run downstairs, reach the corner and the bus pulled up. We knew it would. And we always got there.

—Look, Sarah. If we miss the bus now it's because you're always late. I think you like to keep me waiting, watching you get ready.

—Sometimes I'm ready and you're the last to know.

Or you say just a sec, just a sec, there's one more thing I want to do first. And I'm way ahead of you, just waiting. You don't care.

—You don't let on.

—I don't see why everyone has to groan and carry on like you, complaining. I think you like to wait for me. It makes you a good Boy Scout.

—I'll help my old lady across the street.

—If it bothers you, don't.

—When I go without you, you won't speak—

—As if I cared.

—You don't care if I go or stay?

—You can stay where you are. . . . Poor guy. You don't understand why I love you.

—I can guess.

—Your piercing black eyes?

—More.

—Because you're good right now? Don't smile. You sweet fool.

—You're not pushing me away.

—I know but it won't be so different.

—Oh? Things we've never discovered?

—Do you still have some wild ideas?

—Don't you?

—They would hurt you if I told.

—You can't hurt me.

—I can scare the hell out of you.

—Not now.

—Why don't you give me a baby.

— . . . Too bad to do anything without imagination. Aren't you happy with me?

—We make love once in a while. We work. We have some friends. I'm too busy to think.

—Every day is a new—

—Children when we're old.

—Plenty of time for every—

—If I ever really asked you for something, would you—

—Anything.

—Promise, do you—

—Cross my—

—But don't you want children when we—

—Ssshh. A bird in the hand.

—And we'll have them very fast. We've had so much practice. . . . Don't be angry with me.

—I'm right here.

—I'm always afraid you'll pull away and leave me.

—I'm still here.

—I feel you.

—Everything will work out, girl.

—I'll have gray hair.

—I'll never leave you.

—Now you couldn't if you wanted.

—Don't talk so much.

—You won't forget me? You won't break your promise? You do love me?

—Sneak up closer.

—But look at me! I love you.

—It's all dark, honey. . . .

Suddenly turning, skinning herself in my arms she says —Just give me a baby, lover. And all I can say is —Trust me.

Sometimes I hear what I'm sure is a knock on the door, maybe the grocery boy delivering to the wrong address, a Jehovah's Witness out selling Bibles, or maybe an old friend I've forgotten come to pay a call. But when I reach the door there's no one. Or someone is knocking on the other side of the wall, some kid with a wooden hammer, or a dying old man calling for help, and then it stops. Or there's a tapping on the windowpane until I get up from the table and go into the bedroom to see if someone's on the fire escape trying to get in. Once a pigeon flew away. There's never anyone there. I keep thinking some day there will be.

Playing through my mind like a child teasing me, burning through my body, consuming all other thoughts, she hides in every closet I turn to hide in, waits around every corner, a voice whispering in the dark, I hear things she said in the dark, I remember things we wanted together. And they hurt me. We don't have them.

She bursts through the door with her eyes lit up but cagey, checking that everything is the same between us. She shuts the door, smiling. Her shoes are fish but most of her coat is dry.

—Who walked you home?

—It was just to the corner. She tries to change my mouth with her fingers. She goes to the bedroom and changes into my robe and slippers.

She slaps our supper into the black frying pan, talking with her body, cooing, making our usual mess of chili.

—Come and eat. She watches me come toward her. When she breathes, the robe rises and falls above her plate. I eat. It doesn't touch my hunger. Her hand bunches the muscle of my shoulder and leaves. —Baby, she says, slipping a splinter into my heart. She is silent now with her absolute sureness, smiling at me with some amusing secret. Her legs crossed, her foot swings back and forth nearing me and departing like a pendulum with each stroke drawing us nearer the moment.

I want to take her by the shoulders and shake her and say look woman, I'm nothing right now, I'm no one. I don't have anything to give you. I'm scared and you can't help me.

She rattles and washes the dishes. The bathwater muffles the sound of rain pouring through the gutters. The whole city is being cleansed. The tin bath cover leans against the door. The tub is perched by the sink on its metal legs like a woman holding out her apron. She pins up her hair. She slips off her things from under her robe and puts them beside me on the table for dessert. Her hand comes under my jaw and raises my face, the white wedge of her throat. Hot finger marks on my cheek, her hands move to the collar of the robe she slips off and hangs over my head—flashes of her nakedness and then only the blue tent wrapping me in her scent. The water pounding in the tub stops. I take the robe off.

She looks the same she always does, naked. She steps into the tub, her breasts red apples and her whole body fresh snow melting down into the water.

Drops glisten on her back. A lank of hair slips from its pins and darkens on her neck. Her hands sweep the water to her throat. She catches me watching and I look away. —Won't you catch cold?

—I already have, she says.

—Want to make it worse?

—Would you care.

—I do.

—You'd miss my paycheck . . . I was just joking. She is washing and turning her arms. —Are you only going to sit there?

—Want me to leave?

—No, you haven't had a bath for a long time.

—Last week.

—Liar. I'll be all clean for you, and you'll smell like the subway.

—You used to like the way I smelled.

She kneels in the water with splashing and drops of water catch light all over her skin. —Can you get me a towel?

I leave her to finish and find the towel, and when I come back she rises up in the tub, pouring water, and holds out her hand. Ten feet away I stop and say catch.

She catches. Her breasts juggle my soul. She wraps, tucking the towel between and steps out onto the floor. —Your turn, padding toward me wet footprints, you'll have to bathe alone.

—It won't do any good.

—Feeling sorry for yourself? She unbuttons my shirt with wet hands. I'm not about to have her undress me. I strip my clothes. She watches. I turn away, my legs are thinning. On the side away from her I take a fist of my haunch, slacker than I remember. My arm muscles are running mice instead of city rats under the skin. I shuffle over to the bathtub and climb in warm splashes.

For an instant I hope the water will change me. Down in the warmth I put my head on the bathtub rim and stare at the paint peeling on our ceiling. Waves of slow breathing ripple on my neck and knees. I stir like objects under a murky river. She roughs herself with a towel. Out the window rain patters the roof, tippling into the tin gutters, clogging the drains, rain washing the city air, my home, a cold rain. Pink and white she takes the pins out of her hair. She's bored. She comes and leans against the rim of the tub, red-tipped with her long black hair parting around her. She leans over me. —Not Ground Hog Day yet.

I am, with some effort, up to my chin in water, try- ing to hide under a layer of soap swirls. I can't move.

—Want me to wash you?

—No.

—Where are you hiding the soap? She grapples and finds it. She starts to rub my knees. I fend her off. This delights her. But I have my pride. —What are you worried about, she says.

I'm not sure, so I lie there and she washes me, my knees, my legs, my callused feet, my chest, my shoul- ders. Her hands soothe, pass over me in a clean swathe taking the barnacles off my hull. I could fall asleep. She bends and kisses me.

—Why? I say. I'm acting like a kid.

—Baby, she says. Like white doves her hands settle and hold me.

—Don't call me that.

—What would you like, sweet baby, she murmurs. I reach for her shoulders to kiss her but with a slow rending like the tearing of skin she pulls away. She watches, tense, white teeth, red lips, breathing.

In bed she says —Are you going to say I haven't played fair? Her arm encircles my head. —Did you say your prayers? she says, and her hand offers the apple, so muttering a prayer of the flesh with my lips I give up for the moment most of the years of my life.

I start off to find what I want, groping for a chink in the wall between us I ask and follow her call wandering through carcasses of charred smoldering mattresses, past cars set up on orange crates with their wheels missing, down canyons where rusting fire escapes hang from the walls, pavement sparkling with bottle caps and pieces of tinfoil, red beacon turning on a police car, red flowers opening in a window box, cool alleys where lovers hide in the summer, the smell of vinegar, and blue sky up through the girders of a new building.

And she is all the girls in the city, women I haven't met standing in high windows, in the back yards, pressed close in the subway, memories of her opening the door to me, shedding her nakedness like veils, spreading transparent shower curtains on the city air.

I swing her around, pull her after me, running naked through the streets, a couple of kids in the playground where I grew up, tangled in the jungle gym, strung out on the cool bars, pushing and riding the swings too high, balancing our hearts with the seesaw while grains from the sandpile drift through our bodies.

It can't be like that, married over six years. Flesh thuds against flesh, our sweat smacks of battles. The intake of breath with each moment passes like heartbeats, the ticking of a clock, even if we pass toward something happier than death gulped like a drink of water. Playgrounds are for kids. We aren't so young. On the street I see how young the mothers look, the girls with children while she looks out the window fidgeting, her arms empty. I try to forget children, pleasure isn't play, it is work to forget the feeling which has played tag with me all night maybe all my life as if some memory is there crying to be recognized, made flesh. Glimpses of beautiful things show beyond my reach, and what I lack I was born without, knowing I'll never find it, knowing I'll never love.

So I think then see someone else makes it there, and for an instant I can care for her, plugging into some light socket as her wants and needs pour over me. I can glimpse what it's like to be married to me and not give up. She calls. There is the hope that life will go better, spring will come, and giving up to hope like stepping into the blast from a fire hydrant on a summer day I gather her up in my arms and leap off into a burst of lunch-hour sirens, diesel horns, fuses blowing on the big board, folk songs, and a high wind whistling through water tanks on the roof.

Somewhere on the way down I'm thinking of my parents.

—Let's get married again and do it right, she says.

—We ought to have a kid.

—Don't tease me yet, she says.

We listen to rain in the drainpipes. I'm struck by a disturbing thought. —You do still want a kid?

Her fingers come up and poke my face, forming on my lips and eyelids as though she is blind or deaf, words catching in her throat, and she starts to cry, one or two painful catches at first, breaking into long sobs opening into relief or is she laughing, smoothing my cheek back time after time as if she's soothing away tears there and I am the one crying.

She lies on her stomach with her eyes shut. Only her ankles are covered. Her skin is white as the washbasin. Each buttock is a drop of cold water swelling at the tap. A breast hides under her arm. Her lips are quite red, hair overlapping her neck like billows of black smoke, and through her legs some anonymous lover has clapped a black handful to the intersection. She is my wife.

For our wedding present one of her friends sent us a chopping block with a regular butcher's cleaver. It was a good present because then we bought large joints of beef or lamb wholesale and chopped them into daily portions for Sundays and froze them. She didn't want it in the house at first, and I was afraid to use it when she was in the kitchen. Once I put the cleaver down, washed the beef juice off my hands, and went to lie down until she was through with the vegetables.

I remember the wrong things. I remember an old joke. It's not a very good joke. What do you do when you hurt too much? Jump through a window and put an end to your panes.

I wind the clock and the alarm, try to pick up a penny with my toes, and find myself staring at the utter passivity of her body on the bed. Her flanks are so still they tremble.

—Aren't your feet cold? she says.

Wind sings through the fire escape. I don't dare go to bed. A child will turn out like me. Her body lies with its cheek toward me, half smiling, blinding her own eyes with her lids while I move toward the bed with a curious flutter in my blood. Cushioned on her thighs and buttocks I begin to knead the muscles of her shoulders and back. My hands leave white prints on her pink flesh. Her shoulder blades run like broken birds' wings, lean muscles ripple under my fingers. She on the pillow with her lips apart. We are both objects under the flat glare of the light bulb.

—You lied to me last night, she says.

—You're always scared of what you want, she says.

—Go on, I don't care now, she says.

—You don't understand.

She stretches. —Oh, I understand.

The clock ticks. I am looking at her face sideways on the pillow, waiting for it to change. She moves to accommodate me, lying there awash, her eyes shut tight, a red lipstick print on the pillow.

Inklings come to me in flashes like the stomachs of goldfish. Out of some dark grotto bright blue and purple fish rise toward me, glide in silent schools by my eyes, green and yellow, silver, white ringed with red, until I see a different kind of fish. As I sink deeper the fish lose their color. Shapes with lumps and leeches and blinded eyes hurt to look at. A dark fish covered with spines swells while little bubbles come from its mouth as if it's trying to tell me something, a phosphorescent shark with rows of naked teeth, and coil upon coil of a giant white squid with pods and tentacles grasping blindly through the murky water to touch—

She doesn't realize that we're over, her body moving like water, finding its own form beneath me, on the pillow her smile freezing my soul, bounding against me, twisting around me like a fish trying to get off the hook but hooked, pursing the smile on her lips, hooked until her eyelids flutter and she flees streaking the pillow with her smile.

Death is when the heart stops.

She is wearing blue jeans, a yellow halter and sandals, buying groceries along the avenue. She pushes through to the front of the stand, moving her hands over the pears, lingering, she chooses fruits like a blind woman. She doesn't see me. The vegetable man says don't handle lady to another, while she weighs an eggplant in her palm, squeezes and chooses another, her skin pale against the tomatoes, holding lettuce like a lover's head, her hair free and black as a crow. She smiles. The sunlight hangs about the street in patches. She chooses the summer squash and comes out toward me hugging the brown paper bag like she's in love. Funny things make her happy, she used to say vegetables smelled like the countryside. Then she sees me and stops, and walks down the street the other way alone.

Down the hill through the trees are open spaces lit by the stars. She wants to stop so I pull her mother's car off the road. We stand by the car. The night is big because there aren't any buildings to block it out. I take her hand. We listen to the tree frogs and a dog howling up on the hill. She wants to walk, alongside the road a little and then back into the trees where she finds the path. She knows her way.

There are patches of sky up through the trees and down the hillside patches of water like the sky. The ground is soft. I trip on a root. She goes ahead and pine branches slip back in my face. The air is clean. Mosquitoes are little bastards. The sound of tree frogs becomes just another part of the calm, the crush of my feet on the pine needles and the breeze when it hits the top of the trees.

The turns and black trunks look one like another. She is so sure of her way. We are going down toward the water where the air is damp and cooler.

The smell of mud and old green leaves mixes with

the rich earth hidden from sunlight and the pine needles where the trees reach out over the water. Water laps at the shore. She doesn't say anything but leads me around the pond. A frog splashes.

A clearing of long soft grass. Where the breeze strikes it rustles. The hills rise around us, the pond is flat out into the night with the dark wall of forest on that far shore curving around back to us. Calm black water, the breeze comes off it smelling like the inside of a flower jar back in our apartment when she leaves the flowers in too long.

She unbuttons her dress, walks toward the trees at the water's edge and takes her dress off over her head, slips out of the rest. She's more naked than I've ever seen her with the massive black tangle of pines, the deadwood on the ground, that open space of grass and the whole night sky over us. Her body is soft white while the water is black as her hair, reflecting great folds of the hills around, and up close the jagged pines.

She hangs her clothes on a branch and comes to me. She begins to unbutton my shirt, playing with me, she doesn't care. She wants to go in for a swim. She wants me to go with her. Her feet are white in the grass.

I leave my clothes on a dead branch. She has already stepped in the water, breaking the surface with her long legs. She wades slowly out into the pond, beautiful, cracking the dark reflections, breaking the points of the stars. As though there is nothing in herself or on earth to fear. The slope is gentle enough. She steps slowly without looking back. Her pale reflection shimmers by her body on the ripples. She wades down into the black water with the ripples widening and catching the starlight. She goes into the water like a child.

I stop at the edge. It is too dark under the water. I stand with my feet in the mud. Down in the water is a wavering streak of white which is my body. I look and let the water still. Up past my head are the stars and a shallow black sky. And there motionless is the outline of my face.

She calls for me. She's going on without me. I step, the water's cold. I shiver. Under my feet the mud is mixed with strands of grass. Her body is very white ahead of me, over her thighs in black water. The silence pulls me in, our world is calm. A breeze moves toward us and a dog howls up on the hill and I start to run out toward her, sloshing the water, splattering drops up cold on my stomach and back, and the water churning white around me for a brief rushing instant falls back to the smooth black surface.

Beside her we edge out into the dark. She puts her wet hand up on my shoulder. The slope begins to drop off sharply. Deeper. Her body is clothed in black water, her white breasts rising. She smiles as she used to with her hair black as the rising water. I don't know what she wants. I can't tell what she's looking for. She puts her arms in front of her and gives over to the water closing around her shoulders and neck, taking her away from me.

I'm left alone. I want to scream and break the unearthly calm over the pond. She moves slowly out into the deep water as though there's nothing wrong, her hair trailing behind her, splashed with drops like the stars as her limbs slowly open and close under the water like dull silver gathering light.

I let go and sink down slowly until water is all around me warmer than the air. I push out toward her, swimming slowly after her until we are together, floating. The darkness of the water is part of my body, I'm not sure where I stop and the water begins, I'm free and alive floating free of my body and she is beside me. I'm not scared anymore. I'm okay. She moves slowly out toward the center of the pond, she leads me deeper and deeper into myself until I am no one but part of the water and part of the earth that holds it and part of her. The shores fall away and without limits the pond opens like a great eye under the heavens so we can look up and see our moment's reflection in the stars.

I wake to a soft rapping. I am sure I heard it and look out the bedroom window where the pigeons sometimes fool me, but the fire escape is bare. Rap, rap, soft knocks at the door, I open.

She is wearing a canary-yellow suit. Her hair is pinned up in a wreath. Our eyes are locked on each other and she begins to smile.

—After walking up five flights you could ask me in.

I am blocking the door. As soon as I move she brushes by me into the kitchen smelling of spring outside and her old perfume. She stops in the middle of our lives to take a good look. I follow her eyes. The rough floor needs paint. She bought the blue pot on top of the refrigerator. I am embarrassed by the apron hanging by the stove because it is not hers. Over the stove is the painting of a naked girl yellowed by years of gas fumes. The sink is full of unwashed dishes.

—Everything looks pretty much the same, she says.

I lean against the door and watch her.

She can't stay with my eyes. She sits up on the corner of the table and shifts from one thigh to the other until she's comfortable. Her skirt is high. She crosses her legs at my stare.

—Well? She stretches out her bright arms to me with the crooks of her double-jointed elbows sunny and up, as if we were about to be good friends. —Aren't you glad I came up?

Out the window the sunlight is dazzling, pouring into the airshaft. I want to laugh, just to look at her life is an apple tree and each moment a good red apple. I want to go to the windows and let in spring, the fresh air, a better life, clear the table of dishes and bills and spread her naked out on the hard wood.

—How are the kids? I ask.

She stares back at me until her eyes begin to smart. Then she gets off the table and turns her back to me. —The kids are fine. Joseph's fine. Then she picks up my old coffee cups and with her hand trembling takes them over to the sink.

—All you ever wanted was someone to clean up, she says. She stares down at the dishes piled up in the sink. Then she reaches out and turns on the hot water. The stream splatters on the side of the pot, trickles off the plates. We wait for it to warm. It means she won't leave right away and I'm glad. She stands very still. Her fingers curl an imaginary necklace at her throat.

It takes a long time for the hot water to come up from the basement. I can't take my eyes off her, waiting. She prefers not to look at me now. The water turns suddenly hot, steam rises off the dishes. She adjusts the water taps to bearable, but the water is splashing up on her cuffs so she steps back and by shrugging her shoulders slips out of her yellow jacket. Laying it on the bathtub cover she pulls each sleeve of her white blouse to the elbow. And begins to wash.

She is using a ball of steel wool left on the sink top. I watch her wash a cup with her slender white fingers enmeshed in the steel filaments, and then another. I have forgotten the down on her arms, the straight line of her waist and her long flanks. I have forgotten her stiffness when she is anxious or afraid. I remember the smell of her body. Her breasts look different.

She scrubs each plate with the ball of steel wool until I think she will scrub the paint off. As though we both know in our silence when she finishes if she finishes, something between us will be over and slip into the past, gone again, and she will put on her yellow jacket and pick up her handbag and walk out that door and out of my life again. But I can't say a thing.

I begin to sweat. I hang on every movement of her long limbs which once held me together, explore the dark shadow in the folds of her hair, smile at the impossible angles of her elbows as she washes the inside of the pot, her lips held primly together. She reaches for the silverware and washes each spoon separately, slowly, and rinses each, now turning a long knife over in her hands. She gathers all the knives and forks together in one hand and begins to rinse them again.

—We must be getting old, she says. She turns and faces me holding the knives and forks like a prayer book or something to hold on to, before her with drops falling off her hands to the floor. Her eyes burn me. Her face is hiding a secret. I take a step toward her, but she clasps her hands into her stomach and the water spreads up through her blouse. I step toward her. She hints with her mouth uncertain and when I step again and find her cheek with my hand her whole mask falls away, her fingers spread. Silver rains on the floor. She brings her hands to her face and tries to hide, saying no I'm sorry, I didn't mean that. And she stands away.

—I know. I gather her up against me like the kid I was once with her who could take the whole world up in his palms, choose his love, make his own life, and I hold her, knowing spring after a long winter waiting for my body to remember her to the sounds she makes like memories of pigeons.

It still hurts. Nothing has changed. I can still see her running out of the waves toward me leaving the blue and purple colors of pain, promising. I dream of her always at the moments which should be sacred, when I am beginning to love, the last dream before I wake to some other is her smiling, or in the nights when I pray and desperate make some connection, as though god is playing a fair trick on me.

So I hold her against me, this angular memory with sharp hipbones and full breasts, hot wet cheeks and children by another man, while she cries, and I cry. We weep and uselessly pat each other like strangers looking for something we had and lost until there is nothing left but silence. The moment is never completed, it has never ended. We sit on the table together side by side talking a little, staring out the window. Finally she slips one arm and then the other into the sleeves of her sunny jacket and says it's time. At the door she bangs my shoulder hard with her forehead and is gone. And I start picking up the silver scattered about the floor.

TWO

Silver Apples

Red brick chimneys and black pipes wander off across the roofs toward the church tower. Sun pushes down through the smoke and if you look over the side, green orange and black fire escapes run down all the buildings past potted geraniums, clean and dirty windows, windows with old people staring out at the street, windows with young women, families on the fire landings and below on the street with its junk cars and new cars, the fire hydrant on full blast with half-clothed kids dancing in and out sometimes lifting the jet of water with a piece of tin into a passing car window.

Sarah ties her shirt around her bare waist. She has specks of white in her black hair, on her white wrists and forearms. She's laughing. The four rooms are on the top floor. We paint the walls flat white except for the main room and I paint that deep blue by mistake. We hang rugs over it. We take up the linoleum and leave the wood rough like the country. She has a white mouse which she keeps in a cage and feeds lettuce to, it sniffs about her fingers and hides in the palm of her hand. She hangs a mobile of carved birds by the window. And on the wall by the stove an old print of the Peaceable Kingdom with the sun coming up behind a lot of smiling animals.

Maggie is tall, in blues, denims, and Joe's t-shirts. She can hold very still while everything rushes around her. In their apartment a colander hangs over the sink, there's watercress in the icebox. The floors are red and yellow and the curtains on the windows have roses. You look out their window over the rooftops at the chimneys sticking up, pigeons sitting out there, and sheets flapping like clouds over the alley. They have a big brass bed and a wooden crib for the baby, table and chairs and nothing else except the wooden trunk Joe keeps his tools in. He only showed me what was in the trunk once—he opened it to get a hammer lying near the top and there was every kind of tool imaginable, different sizes, wrenches, ratchets, string, compartments for different-sized nails and hooks and copper wire all mixed together and he shut it again.

Most of the time when I go over to borrow a tool he says just a second I'll get it, and leaves me standing out by the door. He's lithe and strong but small with an open trusting face, thick black hair, black eyes. They're both kids.

I can smell the tar. The black roofs all around us, uneven acres of hot tar. The chimney bleeds a wet black trickle. Sarah slowly turns the pages of the Sunday paper. Maggie holds her baby between her legs on her skirt, sunning. Joe balances on the ledge over the alley.

Joe and I walk up and down the line of march in orange windbreakers. In the evening we stand security at the gates of the campsite, then get a ride back into town where we sleep at the house of a young black girl. She sleeps with her mother and Joe and I get her big double bed. We fight for her attention during the day but she plays us like high-school kids. On the way north we are arrested with three others out on the road. They drive us around back country roads trying to find a jail for us. Joe and I are handcuffed together and they take us out of cars and put us into cars and sometimes it's police officers driving us around the woods and sometimes it's gas-station attendants but they won't tell us what the charges are. In the bullpens when the prisoners are beating us badly Joe calls for help, he calls for help because he's afraid we're being killed and the jailers finally come and laughing order them off us. Locked back in our cells the men swear they will kill Joe in the morning. Joe and I sit there figuring how bad we are hurt. His eyes are dark, they see years beyond me like my father's eyes, he's frightened. And I say don't worry buddy, I won't let them get you. I'll stand by you. I don't know why I say that, unless I am more afraid than he is and can't stand to see it. In the morning, after lying there awake all night the other kids leave the cell when the gates slide back and five or six men come up to our cell. Joe is lying on his bunk swallowing, pale and sweating. I go and stand in the door, shaking, and say you can't come through. They look at me and look at me, then go away. An hour later we are taken to court and freed, and we go home.

The alarm is like a bell signaling the end of a class. I am the instructor. I would just as soon stay in bed but it is my class. It is my daily bread. I don't wake Sarah. In the kitchen I drink my coffee and put the sandwich for lunch in my green book bag and start off through the slums to the university. I call my course words. I never prepare much. I teach what I know. It's getting harder because I know less and less that can be said with words. The course is a search for what is alive, and what is life-giving in the lives we are handed. I teach people to write as they listen to their own pulse. Some can't. Some did once and what they heard scared them too much. They write about their fathers first and lie. And call eachother's lies. Then some write with hatred until that becomes a lie too and they move up toward love again with feeling, alive. In the last paper I ask them to write about the instructor. In the first half they insult me, they can pick up on my most unconscious word or act and turn them back on me like knives, finding my fears, laughing at me until they fall gentle and in the second part they put me back together. The men kid me into pride and the women love me a little and I always come out of the course newer and they come out stronger. And that is my job as I see it.

Sarah used to go to grad school but now she goes to work. It's dull work I guess. She laughs. One of the married guys at her office drives her home on the back of his motorcycle. She wants children. I teach when I can get a job, and write. We see friends. We feed people. Sarah likes people, she likes to be with me with people. We make love. I don't want any kids yet.

Maggie and Joe come into our kitchen for coffee. Joe is saying you can spot a junkie by the way he moves down the street or lifts his coffee cup, the long-sleeve shirts in the summer, he says he can tell by a look in your eye because he was on hard stuff for a year and quit, not that many people quit—it was because of Joel, when he knew Maggie was going to have the baby he got on a bus to Mexico with a ticket and no money, and shook it. It isn't so surprising, Joe has tried almost everything and he isn't too interested in the way people are supposed to do things. His parents live out in the suburbs and would give their lives for him.

When he was seventeen he quit high school to go work with animals. He can talk about animals for hours. He works for an animal man who supplies zoos and sideshows all over the East. Joe is his best handler. Sometimes he brings home a lynx for the night, a monkey or South American bird. He's best with snakes. He brings them by. Dry and glistening they wind amid his fingers. He lets the small ones chew on his hand.

Once he let a big one free and it went over and coiled by the refrigerator until he whispered for it and the snake slithered back to him and wound up his arm. Once in a while something bites or scratches him, not often. He trusts them. He has power with animals. I'm scared of the snakes. Maggie of course sits back cool and proud of him. Sarah laughs delighted. Snakes and evil are part of a game. She handles them at arm's length. But she loves the animals. The night she gave away her white mouse I found her crying in the bathroom. It makes me feel she wants a baby when she handles animals or talks about them like people. When the war started, Joe said he liked animals better than people in the long run.

Sarah and I have the door open because it's so hot and she's cooking dinner for friends. Joe walks by and up the stairs to the roof with a rope coiled over his shoulder. I figure he's going to string a clothesline. But he waves as he goes by the door and smiles some kind of private joke so I sit there thinking about it while Sarah and the people talk until I hear the phone ring over at Maggie's and she bursts out her door and into our kitchen. She stands there with her head down a little, glowering at us, furious. And then she says

Joe's down in the alley. He was climbing down the side of the building on a rope and fell. The landlord called. I run down the five flights and I can hear the commotion down in the alley. The tenants are standing around Joe. He sits there holding his leg. The rope dangles halfway down the brick wall of the building but it runs out about two stories up. His ankle's bent the wrong way. I take off his boot to see if the bone is sticking through—I'm a medic in the reserves—but it isn't. I carry him inside to the stairwell and sit there waiting for the ambulance. He laughs. He says the rope ran out on him and he couldn't get back up it.

When we move to the large apartment we don't see so much of Maggie and Joe. We all live out our lives. The war is coming on strong and I worry about being called up with the reserves. When we see them for dinner Maggie's just the same but Joe is nervous, bitter. He sees something I don't see with his eyes like black beans. A week later I hear he's gone into the hospital with hepatitis.

Sarah and I go over to see Maggie and find her leaving for the hospital. Joe is on the critical list. They have taken a liver biopsy for some kind of experiment in the medical school. And when they take him back to his bed he starts bleeding again. And he starts calling for the nurse but no nurse comes so he gets out of bed and tries to make it to the hall but falls on the floor and he is bleeding all over the floor when the nurse looks in and then goes out again and shuts the door. He screams. Then he passes out. And when they come in and find him they take him down to the critical ward. So Sarah and I take Maggie over to the hospital and wait outside the critical ward for her. She is in no shape. We take her home for supper and put Joel to bed. He's crying and doesn't want his mother to leave him. Joe's sister comes by to spend the night and we take Maggie back to the hospital and Joe's parents are there but only Maggie can go in where all the machines are whirring and lights blinking on the bedside boards keeping people alive. After a while she comes out and starts crying and everyone tries to pat her and tell her it's all right but it isn't all right and she doesn't want it and I'm afraid she's going to break, so I take her up in my arms and let her cry for a while. Then she goes back in.

Joe has been in the hospital for a long time. Maggie goes by pretty much every day. Sometimes I go see him on the way home from work. We talk about going on trips together, doing things. Maggie has drawn a picture for his room of her, naked, with simple lines of her shoulders and breasts and an open profusion of spirals between her legs. He wants to get up. He gets out of the hospital for a while but the animal man won't hire him back so he finds work as a welder. Every morning at six he drives up the river to Maggie's home town where his job is and back to the city every night. Sometimes they take the child and stay with her parents overnight, but he gets too tired and has to go back to the hospital. I take him books to read when I think of it.

Joel is getting older. Sarah and I go see Maggie, and a friend named Norman is there. They have known eachother since they were kids and we all go for a walk after supper.

Once each week we go to see my parents for dinner. You go up a red carpet and at the top of the stairs under a marble table is a Japanese baby made of porcelain with his legs drawn up under him, leaning on his elbows. He is used as a pillow. Past a closet full of wines into the living room and dining room. One wall is glass mirrors. Reaching out from the wall two golden hands hold small chandeliers. There are Lanskoys and Arps on the walls, the walls are green silk. The draperies are green silk and on the floor is a deep purple carpet, and a bright green red and yellow flower print on two chairs and the sofa. A leather-topped desk with a Florentine border, a round table covered with purple velour and a circle of glass, a brier dining table with four Windsor chairs, the two jade obelisks on the mantelpiece, leave a great deal of space to move free in. Sometimes I want to break every piece of furniture in the room. They are my parents. In my way I love them. We have steak with green sauce and wine, always something very special and the finest cut of meat and afterward my father puts some tomatoes and lettuce and squash and bacon, fruit, in a bag for us and at Christmas he puts in a bottle of bourbon and Scotch too. We head home with our booty but I am always hurt and sad after seeing them.

I don't know how Maggie does, except live life as best she can with her baby, shopping and washing the laundry, drawing some, and seeing a few friends.

Friends on the way out and friends who are going to make it through. You keep hoping the ones who are losing and heading out will touch down firm, hit bottom soon and stop. Spring the hell out of here where you can walk down the street and see the knife in a person, a man bent over the headlight of a car holding his stomach, a man clutching his arm with the blood spurting through his fingers, a man with blood running down through his hair walks along the sidewalk as though everything is all right. A kid with glazed eyes dances through the traffic, and the junkie is spread out on the pavement with her arms full of holes and bruises, her body dwindled to a few spikes of humanity, a white girl in a green dress spread out on the pavement this winter day.

Our house is quiet. Around Sarah and me the world wears people down and throws them into the streets. The machinery spits out raw bleeding hunks of flesh with the orange crates and innersprings and the paper bags of garbage in a vacant lot. Sarah comes home from work every night, slips out of her shoes and cooks supper. She grows older.

We try to change our life. I want to find more teaching work. Sarah will quit her job and go back to graduate school if she can get a fellowship or grant. Then we will have something to hope for until my stories sell. She fills out one application after another.

Midwinter the streets are lined with Christmas trees and men warm their hands over the pitch burning in cans. Morley arrives in town and takes us out to dinner. He was Sarah's tutor in college and they have always admired eachother. Sometimes Sarah looks at him with that high glitter reserved for her father. Morley is a curious academic. He was an air-force career officer until he discovered a horror in killing by coordinates and left to join the university. Medium height, medium build, short-cut gray hair, nondescript white face with sharp blue eyes. He has a wife and three children and is now the head of an English department in the Midwest. So. We drink wine and laugh. He says Sarah must go back to graduate school and offers her a fellowship in his department. He says we must come out, the winters aren't bad with good friends.

Spring is coming in. Our friends pair off, shuck their heavy winter clothes. I stop looking at the ground in front of my feet and look off down the block again. My part-time teaching job has turned into a full-time offer for the fall. We run into Joe and Maggie on the street. They have come into some money and Joe looks well. They are renting out on the seashore for the summer. So with spring Sarah and I decide to stay where we are. But when returns start coming in from the graduate schools Sarah is offered no fellowship or grant or scholarship anywhere within the city or without. She is upset. I keep telling her it's all right, everything will be all right. I don't know how. Then one day there is a letter from Morley in the mailbox. She receives a teaching fellowship, free tuition and a grant and at the bottom of the letter in pen Morley has scribbled come and join us.

Sarah is very happy. It's a lot of money. You can spend all your time writing, she says. It's a new start. But I have a job here. I have a weekend with the reserves once a month. She will accept the fellowship and grant and I will work here for a term, then join her with enough money to coast. I can go set her up and join her. If my medical unit is called up she will be all right. We celebrate. I say to my friends you know Sarah's going away in the fall and I'll join her, and they say that's sad why are you doing that. Well a short separation is good.

We visit Sarah's parents on the seashore. Sarah is close to her family and I love them. Their home is a great brown Victorian which is never locked. Her mother sits in the window where the tree stands at Christmas. Downstairs the wallpaper is old green and the carpet is brown. The refrigerator is full of little bowls with radishes and cheese bits, sliced ham, beer, last night's salad. Sarah's old bedroom is on the second floor and in the summer the rain patters the tin porch roof outside her window. In the attic is a box of my old books from college and her father's duffel bag from World War II, packed and ready to go, and a box with Sarah's diplomas in it and letters from her old boyfriends and snapshots. Snapshot: lined up in front of their brown house I see Mr. Thomas the lawyer, short and stocky, even now muscled, sunken breastbone as if his heart were sacrificed, and short white hair like Morley. His hands are folded in front of his sex. Mrs. Thomas is tall and rambling with full spread breasts. She once worked in a dance hall and is holding her breath for fear of saying the wrong thing. Her eyes squint and hold the camera, they have not forgotten anything. The eldest son is thin, wearing a baseball cap, with his toes pointed outward. His face is a vacant storefront, he was killed in the latest war.

The young son is heavily muscled, with the broad genial features of his father. He displays a drunken interest in his mother who stands beside him while he slaps his tummy. Behind her brothers with black hair down over half her face stands Sarah. She is hiding. In a separate picture taken just before our marriage she is standing with her feet apart, her hands around her tiny waist with large white breasts and orange nipples, her hips like loaves of fresh bread. She is grinning. In a picture taken at age eleven by her father she looks like a frightened white rabbit. In a picture taken by her mother she is sticking out her tongue and holding a red pincushion between her legs. The picture taken by her younger brother was taken with the wrong distance setting so the blades of grass in the foreground are incredibly clear while Sarah's body seems an amorphous white glow waiting to distill. Then there is the picture my parents took at their house. I'm in my old leather jacket smiling at the camera. Sarah stands in her purple coat from college looking up at me and laughing, laughing, laughing.

At the seashore we spend our days lying around in the hot sand. Sarah's old man and I go spear-fishing for sea bass, wading into the sea where the surf breaks over and around the rocks, masks and flippers and hand spears along our arms, stretching the elastic tight. On calm days you can lie on the surface and look down for the fish in the shadows, but when the water's full of sand you have to get down and poke around the rocks where the fish dart out like surprises in the green. We usually get four or five and at night Mrs. Thomas cooks them while Sarah and her old man and I sit slapping mosquitoes, drinking, talking politics, or playing sea bass lying under the table croaking for our dinner. Late at night Sarah and I make love like the washing in of a wave and washing out again. I tell her we will have a child when I join her in the Midwest.

Maggie and Joe are out on the Cape, they have a house on the town waterfront. We wait in the kitchen for them to come home, until Maggie bursts through the door so fast I'm not ready for her and we're hugging and kissing and Sarah and Joe are hugging until I stop and hit him on the shoulder and laugh. He looks pretty well but there is something he sees that makes his eyes grow dark and sad.

We sit and smoke, sip whiskey and talk until the music stops playing upstairs and you can hear the water lapping up on the beach. Maggie stands and stretches and says she wants to walk. So we all set off down the sand past the other beach houses with their lights off and the stars are sparkling up in the empty spaces of the sky. There isn't any surf, the black water just pushes up against the sand and gives up and pushes again and gives up until about halfway down the beach the girls wade in and Maggie says we should go in swimming. Sarah takes my hand in the dark. I say we should go in swimming because the night is beautiful and the water is. Joe says okay but back toward the house because he sure is sleepy and Sarah says so we can get our bathing suits. But we don't get our bathing suits. We stand in a huddle on the sand feeling the fresh breeze and getting around to unbuttoning our clothes. I step back not to crowd Maggie who is slipping off her dress and Sarah stands by me watching me unbuckle my belt not knowing what to do with her hands. I kiss her and say it's all right and she begins to take off her blouse. Maggie is free first and stands with her thin back to us waiting for Joe to step out of his pants. Then the four of us start for the water like a ragged flight of duck. Maggie is tall and thin with untanned strips of skin brilliant against the water. All of Sarah is pale, trying to hide her breasts with her forearms, and Joe is running out into the water for cover. Maggie laughs. The water's too shallow for us to hide from eachother. We look at the sky overhead and listen to the night and wade with mud and seaweed between our toes and the low-tide water up to the crooks of Maggie's knees, four naked bodies looking for deeper water. When the water is up to the backs of her thighs we slip down. Sarah hangs on my neck and tries to stay underwater, while Maggie and Joe drift several yards away. There's absolutely smooth water all around me and my wife's arms around my neck, her breathing moving the water, Maggie's laughter, and that's all. We come out and wet slip on our clothes. Back at the house Joe pulls a mattress off their bed and gives it to us. We all sleep in the kitchen because kids have rented the upstairs and a family's staying in the next room.

We run into a boy and girl who know Morley. The boy is a graduate student at the university. He is in the same department and has a teaching fellowship too. They are living together because they don't believe in marriage. They know Morley very well. The winters are long. The girl who had the fellowship and grant Sarah is taking over was Morley's mistress. They had a love affair all winter until the girl left school and went home to Australia. They say Morley is very much a lady's man. I go out on the porch and leave them to talk. Afterward Sarah says whether it's true or not it doesn't have anything to do with us. I tell her I don't want her to go. She says I'm a raving lunatic.

Maggie moves from table to stove. She washes her face, dresses her kid, makes us coffee like a dancer with her breasts moving free under her blouse. She takes off the purple bandanna and brushes her hair. She looks away. The kids come down from upstairs for coffee and Maggie's brother and his girl come out of the next room late for breakfast as usual. Maggie is talking and laughing. She stands behind Joe's chair with her hands in his hair. When she laughs she shows all her teeth in a grin. And when one of the guys challenges her she lifts her chin. She says nothing to me all day, but she passes me the sugar first for coffee, touching my fingers when I give her matches, noticing my eyes on her breasts without flinching, smiling right at me as she laces her cool white fingers in Joe's hair. Sarah looks at me sarcastically. Joe isn't paying any attention, used to guys looking at Maggie. I don't push her or say anything. Maggie doesn't give me any opening. There's a kind of electricity there and every now and then we brush or touch and it's hard. Outside Maggie lies in the hammock with her skirt folded up in her lap and long legs brown in the sun. I play with Joel. Sarah goes out swimming alone, and Joe lies like a stone in the grass.

Maggie and Sarah take Joel off to do the laundry together and the kids upstairs start a party on the side lawn. Joe and I sit on the basement cover sipping gin, though he isn't supposed to drink anymore. The kids are all ages. The woman next door brings over the gin and walks among us in her bikini pouring drinks. Her daughter lives with one of the boys upstairs. Her husband takes off his shirt in the sun. She puts down the empty pitcher and cups a boy's hand with both of hers as she lights her cigarette. An older kid rests his arm around her bare waist. Her son sits up on the hood of the car and watches his mother, while someone's three-year-olds wander in and out between bare legs. Then Sarah and Maggie are standing there with the laundry bag between them and Joel. I say, let's go get some supper, and Joe says we ought to take some blankets and sleep out because the party isn't over yet. So the girls gather up some blankets and sweaters and we leave without anyone really noticing except the boy on the hood of the car when we ask him to move. We buy corn at a roadside stand out of town, and barbecued chicken and beer at a shopping center. We drive to the beach where the dunes run too far along the coast to patrol. With the sun sinking behind us and the sky light gray blue over the water, we walk with the blankets trailing on the sand and the grocery bag splitting, with Joel laughing in Maggie's arms, until we find a stretch on the water shielded by sand hills. Joe and I make a fire of driftwood. We spread a blanket. And when the flames die down Joe douses the corn, husk and all, in salt water and lays the pieces on the coals. We eat and drink, looking out at the high breakers hit hard and just the water as far as you can see. The dark comes in and there are stars and our fire and the glow on our faces, and the wind takes everything from my mind I don't want to think about. I joke with Joe and play with his kid. We lie around the blanket and tell Joel stories about Indians and how they cook corn in the husk, until Maggie wraps him in a blanket. Sarah kisses him goodnight and tells them we're going to have a baby too when we get settled. Until there is just the four of us looking up at the stars or the flames flickering on eachother against the black ocean and the full harsh sound of the breakers.

Maggie passes me the beer can. Sarah is pressed along my side. I take the beer can and press my hand over hers, my fingers slip between hers to the metal. When she leans back her elbow digs into the sand by my arm. I know Sarah is looking at me, lonely. I look at Maggie, caught by the fire flickering fingers of light over her face. I shut my eyes. I trust Sarah. I trust Joe. The breakers are hitting the beach. I stand up and say I'm going in swimming, doesn't anyone want to come in swimming with me, but no one says anything. Joe nods his head and puts his arm around Maggie's shoulders. I walk away from the fire and strip. The three of them lie together beyond the flames. I run away down toward the water where the sand turns hard and run several steps into the wash when the first wave hits me and I plunge down into cold water. A wave breaks over me. I swim in blackness. I get up in the wind suddenly with salt in my eyes suddenly scared of the water until a swell lifts me and I swim again, one arm over the other, catching my breath, trying to swim away from that calm in me which tells me I'm married and I love Sarah or if I can't always love her hurting her slowly kills me. I try to swim away and I swim until my shoulders ache and I have no more breath for the rough water. I make it in through the breakers and come out on the sand. Our fire burns far off down the beach. The wind begins to dry the salt on my skin. I shiver and start back. —Joe says it sure must have been cold. Sarah chafes my back through the sweater. Maggie stands several steps away smiling at me, and while Joe hugs Sarah good-night Maggie tucks the blanket around Joel. We all lie down together with our feet at the fire. Sarah burrows in the hollow of my arm. On my other side Maggie turns her back to me under their blankets. I take a cool handful of sand in the space between us and stare up in the sky at the points of light, nameless, number-less, like the grains of sand slipping through my fingers or the faces on a crowded street.

The sand is cold. The fire's out. The wind has turned the blanket back and sand is in my clothes, in my hair, stuck to my cheek. Sarah is hidden under the blanket and my arm. Her breaths are like the steady crash of the breakers. The black dunes and Maggie and Joe's blanket beside us. But the stars are awake and wind moves along the beach. I stretch my fingers in the sand and run my hand through it like a girl's hair. I want something in that whole crowd of stars and streets filled with strangers' faces. I stare at a cold star afraid. I would give anything for Maggie to put her hand out in the space between us. Sarah breathes in the shelter of my arm and overhead the star I'm searching grows warm and distinct, the other stars grow warm as Sarah's breath, spreading their points of light out toward eachother until they run together in my eye. In the morning we leave. Maggie and Joe are going to Mexico in the fall.

Back in the city there's my weekend reserve duty. I put on my starched medical whites and take the six o'clock subway out under the river. The subways smell like the old men's ward. I help a man off the toilet when he has a heart attack and carry him to his bed and wait for the defibrillator and a foreign doctor who sticks a long needle between the ribs looking for heart, saying missed, missed. We wrap the body in a plastic sheet, tag the toe and wheel him down to a tray. In the summer the smell of dead rats seeps out of the cellars of tenements around and I confuse it with the smell of the drunk tank and mental ward through the series of locked gates in the basement, past piles of old mattresses. They strap a man's feet to his bedposts when he goes into the d.t.'s but he bounces up and over his feet and cracks his skull on the floor. A black woman asks me to pray for her.

In the strange city Sarah and I stay in a hotel and watch television half the night. We find a ground-floor apartment in a small brick house and move in the stuff we brought up. The rent is good. There's a yard out back, and there are flowers by the porches and steps.

I build a wooden platform for the bed and set the mattress in so there is a table at one end. I put shelves up for all her books, and locks on the windows, extra latches on the doors. I put her desk under the shelves. We paint all the walls flat white in our bedroom, the floors are thin strips of polished hardwood. From yards and yards of green burlap she makes curtains. There is a little room I'll make into a study when I move up. I stack all my books in there. Sarah gets a dog, a big collie about half as big as me. We call him Buddy because his former owner has already named him. So Sarah is settled in. We see Morley and his wife and children for dinner. Morley and I are standing alone with our glasses and I tell him what we heard this summer. Reddening, he looks at me with that hard blue gaze as though I am part fool. He says only it will be good when I come out to join Sarah. Everything will be all right. I leave.

In my room there is a typewriter, a telephone, gated windows to keep the robbers out, a bed, stove and sink, a picture on the wall of Dionne Warwick—a poster of the concert Sarah took me to on my birthday, a Valentine she made for me once with arrows through the names of publishing houses, a string of beads and my dog tags.

It's fall, and I run into Maggie on the street. She and Joe are leaving soon for Mexico. We have a hot dog together but we can't meet with our eyes.

When I go to see Joe he's pale and thinner, still set on moving to Mexico. The war goes on. He says Maggie's down at a peace march in Washington, her friend Philip went with her. Joe wasn't feeling well enough. When he's rested they'll leave for Mexico.

Joe and Maggie and I go out on the ferry together. There's a music concert on board. We listen. I have trouble keeping my eyes off her. I feel pulled to her. They are going away. Joe is my friend. Out on deck when the ferry touches the far shore Joe turns away and looks out into the night. I say, I'm going to miss you, I'll miss Joe too. That's all, it isn't very much. She smiles, confused. We stop for coffee on the way home and I spill coffee on her dress.

The last time I see them I'm serving two weeks' duty at a military hospital in Washington. There is a heavy casualty load from the war so they send us down to unload planes in the middle of the night. I rig my duty hours so I can fly home to teach twice a week and be back in Washington for the night shift. But I have an hour before my plane leaves and I go to say goodbye, they're leaving in the morning. Maggie's next door with her friend Philip and Abby. Joe and I sit in his kitchen. We all used to sit there but it seems a long time ago. We don't say anything for a while. Finally I square off and face him and say Joe my friend. I like your woman. I like your woman too much. He smiles, embarrassed with a private joke, and says I know. I say, if you weren't my friend I'd try for her but it wouldn't do me any good. He just laughs at me, not cruel. He's pleased. Somewhere along the line he's grown wiser than I am.

I don't know why I said anything but I want to tell him something because it hurts me that I want her and would fight him for her. And he is my friend. I am sitting there in my dress uniform with my sergeant's stripes on, my little silver buttons shining down the middle of my blues, here in the midst of the slums, and I have my shoes shined and my stripes on and I am about to go back to Washington and take those men in pieces off planes, change the bandages, men who are younger than my students. I say Joe, take care of yourself man, goodbye. I don't think I will see him again. He gets up and says shucks and slams his hand into mine and taking my elbow we say goodbye and walk into the other apartment to join Maggie and Abby and Philip whom I can't stand with a slightly bent shoulder, hovering nearby with his false grin. Maggie sees. No one talks about my uniform. Everything slides around in my mind and shifts so I am a symbol to them instead of a person but sorting it out I can't see what I stand for. What I can see is that now we are all going in different directions, Sarah and me and Maggie and Joe. I will be lonely. I say well I'm going to catch my plane. I look at Maggie and Joe and say if you ever want anything or need anything, ask me, not knowing what I have left to give but wanting to say that I love them. I hug Maggie, shut my eyes for a second. It is a real goodbye, more than Sarah, because I can't feel anything. I just hug her and press her against me. Then I say goodbye. I hug Joe. I go out and catch the plane.

I was about one and a half when my sister got sick and my mother took her away. They lived out West in the mountains for a year. I don't remember it at all except the feeling of emptiness.

We unload the planes, change the bandages, parcel medication. Wounds. What can you say about wounds. They make me tired. I unbuckle the straps from the litters and put them into bed. I take care of what I can. The bandages are white and yellow and red. There is a smell in the bandages. The sponginess of the bandages makes me very tired, walking across fields of rubber. Men who have lost arms and legs, pieces of them are gone, but they are still men, they just don't have an arm or a leg and that becomes part of the rest of their lives.

Maggie stands staring at us like some trapped animal, goat-like the way her head is tilted and her blue eyes hold us, and says the landlord has phoned and Joe is down in the . . . She sits on a chair in our kitchen, with her legs crossed and her back straight and her chin just a little high, motionless, alive, with her high wide cheekbones and narrow chin and her stringy brown hair down around her ears to her shoulders. Silent. Sometimes she is kind of goofy, elbows and knees, sudden big teeth when she grins. Quiet. . . . She cuts her hand and comes over to our apartment and I wash it and bind it.

Up the river from the city there's an old factory town. Patchwork, wooden houses and a waterfront with barges and houseboats. Joe wants to live there some day with Maggie and his kid. Joel will go to school there. Joe can earn his bread as a welder again. The three of them in jeans, Joel up on Joe's shoulders with his fists in black hair, and Maggie three feet away tapping blades of high grass dreaming she's somewhere else, walking down by the water with the river smell, rats, tar on the barges, rotting wood, rusty winches, and back through the town of gas stations and auto body shops, where the kids she went to school with stand in the doorways of bars. It's her town though she grew up on the outskirts where the artists and teachers live. Her old man has the face of a Kansas farmer and drives the parkway to the city each morning, watches the sun come up through the girders of the high bridge. Her mother draws pictures for children and works in the garden turning over the soil to fresh earth with careful serene hands. Their old farmhouse has wide plank floors, the nails are wooden pegs, a wall is lined with books of American history, the labor movement, Zane Grey and Dreiser. On the other walls hang pictures of each of them painted by eachother. There's a picture Maggie did of herself in a bridal gown with Joe holding the baby.

Maggie, wrapped in her grandmother's quilt with one breast bare, raises her flag with one skinny arm and leads her army—a Valley Forge of gas-station attendants, kids in souped-up cars, Puerto Ricans down from the hills where they wintered on squirrels and magpie, street kids, scarred love children, motorcycle mechanics, dropouts, bears and lovers. Maggie like the spirit of the country sings in the abandoned mill, hovers over the rocks and woods, blows cold through the bare branches over the snow and where the ice parts over the rushing white water of a brook.

I call Sarah one night from the ward. She is miles and miles and miles away. She says she is okay how am I, and she says I have to come up and see her next time since she came down to see me the last time. But she's too far away from me. She's too far away.

After the military training I am frozen very cold and I think I am a little crazy. I keep thinking of the people on the streets, my students, the professors, my friends, with wounds. A girl gives me dinners over at her apartment and one night I lie down with her but we don't sleep together. I can't feel anything. I give her a box covered with seashells, full of green buttons. She gives me a lucky piece she made from an old medal.

Sarah drives me in from the airport in the dark. I keep the scarf high around my neck because the girl has bitten me but at a stoplight she pulls it down to look. She is ironic with me, teasing, sharp. In the apartment the dog jumps all over me and she takes me to bed and warms me until I make love to her. I don't talk to her about the wounded.

We go by her office on the top floor of a fieldstone building. Eaves slant down around a window which looks out into the bare branches of a tree. The dog curls in his place under the desk. The top is bare except for a green book and pad of white paper. Morley's office is down the hall by the water cooler but he doesn't give her any trouble she says. We talk to her friends. We go to the movies. I walk the dog. We make love and sleep and she drives me to the airport.

At Christmas Maggie and Joe send us a letter at Sarah's. In Texas, they are about to cross into Mexico. They are staying with friends of Joe's, and all is well. They think of us.

I am with Sarah when there is a sudden step up in the war. We hear on the radio that the reserves are called up. Sarah's friends say I should stay, they will take care of me. I know what Sarah thinks. I know the war is wrong. But no man is better than his own people. Something breaks in me when I fly home. It doesn't matter so much whose uniform I wear, I will take care of the wounded, and I will take care of my own first. But there will be a price to pay. I find the medical units around us are called but ours is left ready.

I stay with my people. I teach my classes in a daze. One evening Joe's mother calls and says Joe is sick, badly sick, and they are flying home. She wants to use my address so they can get him into his old hospital where the doctors know him. I say sure and hang up and forget about it. Maggie and Joe are far away now and I lose Joe amid other wounds. I telephone Sarah every night, trying to talk to her, but there isn't much to say.

I eat alone at night, dinners of stuffed cabbage and pirogi with Coke at the Polish restaurant on the corner. I don't see much of friends. I don't go to see my parents anymore. I don't like their fresh tomatoes and steak with sauce béarnaise anymore. They don't know anything about shot-up people with their silverware sets and service where each plate could buy a family a week of food. I'm almost finished with my job and I'm ready to leave. . . .

Late afternoon. Sun slants through the windows. There's a knock on my door and when I open Maggie stands there. I sink inside, I don't know how to handle Maggie now. In some way she has come too late for me like a miracle at my door when I no longer hope. And I don't want her pain, or Joe's. I look at her and say come in. I ask her how she is. But she can't seem to focus, she isn't there in my room with the scattered papers and dust and gates on the windows. I give her some coffee and tell her to sit in the only chair and she says Joe is badly sick. It started when they crossed into Mexico, not bad at first but at the end he was unconscious and his legs and stomach were swollen. And she had him flown back on a stretcher. He is in the hospital, and I ask where, but she doesn't know the name, she can't remember the name, only how to get there, and I ask her where Joel is and she says he's with her parents up in the country. She doesn't want to hold any one thought for long. I try to be gentle with her. I don't talk to her about me. She's in pain. She says things, remembers things when the thought strikes her. She says she and Joe had broken up. They had bad times before where he had left or she had left but this time it was over. That's when he got so sick.

I don't know. When you're in pain you look at the world as if everybody else is in pain too. It's hard because there are no easy rules in pain or in escaping pain, like a heart beating. It was easier to look at hers. Everything she said and every breath she took hurt me. Her look was a kind of vacant stare into the future straight ahead, and not daring to look from side to side hurt me, and her confusion for knowing so little about Joe, for not being able to tell me really how he was, for being afraid to talk about it hurt me, though I guess that told me in a way so I said next time she came in she should come and see me and bring Joel and I would take them out for ice cream or a movie and I sent my love to Joe and I kind of put her out the door.

One day Maggie appears again with Joel. I give him some watercolors to play with on the floor while Maggie and I sit on the bed and drink tea, staring out through the thick dust-covered glass at back tenements and yards. She is better. Joe is conscious again. She says she takes Joel to see his father twice a week. She says it is hard for her seeing him now because it is over, though she stayed with him in Mexico when he got so sick, taking care of him. I give her books to take to him, and write a note on the inside cover. She says in Mexico, on the way down, driving, Joe said if anything happened to him, if there was an accident or he got sick again, she should be careful of herself and Joel, and find someone who was worth her, like me.

Maggie stands at the door alone, looking in at me, and I reach out and gather her up and hug her like the time at the hospital but this time we lie down on the bed under the window and kiss and make love. Something in me melts. There is no order left in the world and we strike out toward eachother swimming through her blindness, pain, my numbness, trying to grasp and hang on to the wave rising in us that breaks up through us.

Afterward, after the heat is quiet, and I realize I can lay my hand along her bare skin again, and again, I sit up and say listen what about Joe, what about Joe? I'm suddenly frightened. You've broken with him. She says yes, we're going to live apart, we're not together anymore, it's all right. He was my friend, I say. —I'm no one's woman.

I wonder what he was thinking on the way to Mexico. I ask her what it was like. I see them driving down through Texas in their old gray Dodge, the back seat built into a platform with their things in it and on top knapsacks full of clothes and denim and Maggie's long-sleeved silk shirts and Joe's blue t-shirts and blue jeans. And somewhere in among all the luggage his .22 revolver and his tools. An extra can of gas. Beating the old Dodge over the roads fifty sixty miles an hour with Joe driving driving, not stopping, tired by the summer driving until they reached a town in Mexico where Joe dug up an old friend who ran a garage. They settled in a small town, in a white hut with white plastered walls and a dirt floor, and a woman came in to take care of Joel so Maggie was free more. I think of the designs in tin cans with holes punched in them letting the light through in patterns, and wooden beds and straw mats, and a bar down the street. They lived there while Joe got sicker and sicker though I guess now he wasn't too well when he went —quiet, withdrawn, intense. He was feeling low she said and they were getting on eachother's nerves, and each of them spent more time alone and when they were together fought and got nowhere until finally they sat down together on the bed one day and Maggie said you know we're—there's nowhere to go now. And he said I know, watching her, and then he got very much sicker kind of quickly and she stayed taking care of him—it is hard to see the story clearly. I don't know how she took care of him. There were visits to doctors and medicine and she stayed there though I know at one point she went for a trip about a week alone because she couldn't stand it, and then came back. It's hard to imagine her then, was she angry at his sickness or was her heart breaking, waiting. I don't know what her life was like. Clouded. Men on the streets would make remarks to her even when Joel was with her because she didn't live as their women lived. And Joe was flat on his back a lot and couldn't protect her. But mainly I see them in their room, Joe falling sicker until his legs and stomach began to swell. And somehow she packed their things and gave the car to a friend and got them on the plane and brought them back to America. She says she stayed with him just because he was sick but I'm not sure that was true, love doesn't stop.

We sleep. I wake up to her. It's like throwing myself on ice when I'm burning. I think she's everything I ever wanted.

We go out for supper. On the way to the restaurant she says what are you going to tell Sarah? She looks at me, her head tilted slightly, her eyes a little sharp. I don't know what I'm going to tell Sarah. I don't want to tell Sarah anything.

While friends are away Maggie stays at a loft on the other side of town. I haven't seen her for three days. The big loft runs the whole length of the building. A giant yellow sunflower hangs over the door, the gas heaters burn with a blue flame. It's as if nothing ever happened between us. We are frightened, reserved. There is little to say. I buy her groceries. She makes dinner. Joel falls asleep in an alcove of blankets and quilts. I ask how Joe is and he's better. She knows the name of the hospital. She's seen his parents. She moves about the stove and table with the supper. I sit with my hands folded on the table, crackling inside. Dinner. We smile at eachother. The long yellow floorboards stretch to the far brick wall, the sunflower turns slowly in a draft. After dinner we lie down on blue cushions in front of the gas heater and watch the open flames and take off our clothes. She takes me into her. She is taking care of me, husbanding me, wifing me, and everything in me that hurts and cuts me up inside turns easily into warmth, thanking. At first, making love with Maggie isn't so different from talking with her. We look at eachother's eyes. I say I want to have children, our children. Kids with Sarah, not having them, not wanting them, putting them off. With Maggie I understand wanting kids. Something in me falls apart, shattered. I believe in beauty.

Leaving, looking at her on the mats, the blue cushions around the flames, leaning on her elbows looking at me leave. With her head tilted slightly, stubborn, looking up at me, eyeing me, wondering how the cards will fall but waiting, very sure of something, watching the thread unravel and unravel. I am singing inside, joyful.

I fly out late at night. Big jet. Leaving the plane, working through customs, large empty modern airport, knowing Sarah will be waiting for me outside customs with the dog on the leash and her purple coat sort of smiling at me with her arms open to welcome me home. And so there she is and she hugs me and welcomes me in and we start back to the apartment. I am a knot inside myself. She asks how Joe is, and why I've been strange on the phone, and I say he's okay, getting better now. We start our week together.

I am kind of dead inside, because my pain is alive and Maggie is alive and my wounds are alive. Out here they're all shoveled over with snow, so I walk the dog a little and try to feel out Sarah's life a little. I can't talk to her. I don't have anything I can say. Things begin to wind tighter and tighter. At night in my sleep I wake up calling Maggie, Maggie. Sarah wakes up and asks me acute questions and I tell her to stop hurting me but she keeps asking. She is very cool, kind of humorous about it. She has a better angle on me than I knew. She has more control. During the day it is impossible. I just grow harder and harder until I can tell her I'm getting tied up with Maggie but I don't know what it means and we have a fight and I tell her I'm going back. I call the cab company and wait. And pack a few of my things, my shaving kit, three or four of my favorite books, some clothes, leaving all the pictures and treasures of our life, and put what I have in a suitcase and say goodbye to her as she finally starts crying and I go out the door into a taxicab and weep like a baby, unexplained, all the way through little back streets and out onto the highway. Our big decisions, we ought to know what we're doing. I don't. I only know I have to leave, so I leave.

I go over to Maggie's loft and we make love again. Making love to her is like nothing I've ever known before.

I'm working at my desk and Joe calls up. Who's this? He says Joe. Hi Joe, how are you? He says oh I'm okay, just wanted to call up. Did you get the books, I say, the books. And he says yeah but I don't have much time to read but I wanted to call up and find out how you are. I say I been seeing something of Maggie. He says yeah I know, she's told me. And how's Sarah, what does she have to say? I say I guess she's okay, I don't know, she'll be all right. And I tell him to get well and to take it easy and then there isn't much more to say right now, so he says goodbye. But why did he call? The phone call was touching in, I guess. Knowing why I didn't go up to see him. His voice sounded far away and a little like he was speaking in a tin can, but resonant, echoing. I guess he'll be out soon. I wonder if he still loves Maggie. I guess he'll always love Maggie.

I decide to be alone for a while and go and tell Maggie I'm taking off to clear my head out. She says, some more? I go out to Block Island for three weeks. It's midwinter, my job is over. I stay in a rooming house and afternoons I go out and walk along the beach with the wind pushing me around. Sarah calls me up and says she's visiting her parents and she wants to fly out and see me, but I say I don't know anything, I don't want to see her, I just want to be alone. The days pass. Maggie, Maggie, Maggie.

When I go back to the city her friends are in their loft and Maggie's out in the country with her parents, so I drive out immediately without calling and she opens the door herself as if she's expecting me after three weeks. Her eyes are wide open and she's very pale. I wonder if it shows on my face I want to leave Sarah and live with her. I feel strong enough for that. I hug her and say glad to see me?

She looks at me and says Joe died last night. As if a bomb explodes in me. We walk in the living room and sit on the floor. I can't feel anything. All I can think is that this will finish us and it mustn't finish us, I won't let it finish us. I say it's going to be hard for us, how are we going to make it through. How can we get past Joe's death. I know I love her, I know she loves me. Nothing is going to take me away finally from what I've searched for, dreamed of and paid for with almost everything I have. I can't feel anything about Joe's death. He died. It's like a curtain coming down, a gate slamming, my exit gate.

It is a strange night. Her parents are away. She's in shock. I finally realize she's in trouble, barely holding on to the earth, like she was the first day she came to see me. I try to comfort her. I hold her. She runs her hands over my back as though she has to take care of me. She smiles. She says she doesn't feel anything, she will make dinner.

She says she was going to see him a couple of times a week, but stopped the last week I was away. She didn't think I was coming back. She sat by the window of her midtown hotel and didn't do anything. She had nothing. Joel took care of her. She didn't see him when he died. But the day before she wrote him a poem and sent it to him with Joel when Joe's parents came to take him to the hospital. She did not write poems. The poem said everything she wanted to say and he read it before he died. Yes, she says it was a love poem kind of, he read it before he died.

I say he couldn't die, he was getting better. She says Joe is gone. I hold her. I try to warm her. She can cry some. We go out for a walk. We drive out into the state forest and get out of the car and walk. There is a big moon out and the firs cast shadows on the snow. There's no one else for miles and miles around. I want to jump for the moon, parts of me are floating up toward the moon, catching on the different stars. Somewhere off in the night there's a gunshot and suddenly my whole body is screaming and falling, plummeting down through the emptiness. Maggie beside me looks scared and pale. Her eyes wide open looking at me as though I can do something for her. I take her hand. Back at the house I'm still frightened, in a panic. She holds me and rocks me. I tell her I love her more than anyone in my life, I love her, I'll take care of her. She says but I'm going to hurt you, crying. And I say do you mean you'll leave me, we can't be together, we won't last? She says no, I won't leave you. But I don't understand why she says she will hurt me. She just takes me in her arms and warms me, slowly warms me into sleep.

The minister knows all of us. But no one knows we are together but Joe. His parents are there. I haven't seen them since the time Joe fell off the roof. His sister is there close to Maggie and Joel. Some of his friends are there, and all his parents' friends. I have a hard time staying together and sit in the back. After the service I'm entering a group of mourners at the church door when Joel reaches out of some relative's arms and hugs me, and I hold him for a second but he's taken away. Maggie is standing alone amid the family while people come up to her and hug her. The bells of the suburbs ringing they are sorry. Maggie stands there like a statue. She isn't crying. Joe's parents are weeping and hugging her. And she smiles and pats their backs and tries to comfort them, how many years did she feel and see it coming. I walk past her out of the church and start down the street, then turn and go back through the people to her. The minister stands beside her. I say I'm sorry, and, I wanted to run away but I couldn't. I'm sorry, Maggie. I'm sorry Joe's dead. I kiss her cheek and she kisses me. Then I leave. They are all going out to the graveyard, all the family. But if I could live that over again I would take her away to some park and let her weep for Joe and weep.

It's warmer. We walk down the street together and she opens like a flower. People smile at her. In stores they turn to look at her smiling. They take care of her. They're gentle with us. Everywhere Maggie looks she frees beauty. She looks at the lines of buildings and looks at color. I see colors with her. And breathe. I see flowers. I never looked at flowers before or people's faces. People's faces lose their hardness and they take care of us.

I still don't understand that Joe is dead. We don't talk about it. I don't understand what death means, unless it means that finally there is an absence where you can't say you're sorry. It's final. There's nothing more to be said. It closes a book, it closes it badly or it closes it well but it's closed, and all the things you wanted to say to someone have been said or will never be said. It's strange with Joe because I told him I wanted Maggie, and he told her on the way to his death she should find someone like me. Those aren't things you're supposed to say. And he called me up to ask about it. To find out if I was going to take her and the child over. Not trying to persuade me not to but saying well if that's what's going to happen. He died about a month after that phone call. He didn't sound that bad on the phone, he sounded tired. Maybe he called to find out if his friend had really taken over his woman while he lay sick. But she had told him. Or was it to hand her over to me and say it's all right. But things I didn't say. What didn't I say to Joe. What didn't I say. I should have known he was going down. Of course no one told Maggie, everyone said he was getting better and you know she grasped at that, though his parents knew. The doctor said the damage was irreparable, he thought they should know. And Joe must have known lying there staring up at the ward ceiling, twenty-four, black hair, black mustache, black eyes, being fed with a spoon, then nourishment into his veins. It's hard to know what keeps a man alive. Maggie held him a long time, and she kept him off dope for the most part. Maybe she replaced it, seeing beauty like crystals in the mash of the slum. Maybe all a man needs is hope. He had his wife and his child and that was his life. Now the doctors say they told him not to travel but to rest. He told no one. Was Maggie supposed to make his journey with him.

I took Maggie blind but I took her. And he died. And I suppose the thing I want to say to him is I'm sorry. —He was so damn competitive all the time always fighting it out but it was all out front. And I was that way too and we could fight things out and he could be stubborn and obstinate and a really stupid S.O.B. sometimes, but so could I, we could count on eachother. Until he got sick. The other thing I wanted to say to him and never will was that I loved him.

Maggie and Joel and I go stay at her parents' house in the country where all the joints of wood fit neatly into eachother and nails are wooden pegs, the furniture is old and wood, the fireplace is brick, and everything has its place and belongs in its way where it is. I sleep downstairs on the sofa. I guess they realize we are a little crazy and they are gentle with us. Her mother has beautiful eyes, serene hands, serene hands. As spring comes in she turns over the soil for her garden, always gentle with me, kind of joyful with Maggie, her eyes look like she is in love too, believing in love, believing in joy when it happens, she is a calm believing woman.

I write Sarah a letter saying Joe has died and I'm going to be with Maggie now, and I love her but I don't want to be with her anymore. She comes into the city and has a party for all our old friends. I hear her life is set up, she has new friends, her studies and her job at the university. I guess I set her up as well as I could to leave her. And my own friends treat me like a madman. My friends with money don't call. My parents call me a fool. Joe's parents don't speak. Maggie and I have eachother and Joel, and her parents. We're still falling.

I find work tutoring in the city. We take a loft and start fixing it up. We patch the ceiling with plaster and the brick walls with concrete, install electric wiring and repair the plumbing and paint it all, and sand the floors, Maggie and Joel and I working together. Joel is six. He has a frightening sense he has done something wrong because his father died. I try to teach him he hasn't. There are nights in the loft we get into bed and Joel lies awake around the corner of the partition toward the other end of the loft. And we wait for him to sleep before we make love. Then her body is coming aware to me, then she is trembling ready to accept me completely and give over, and as though Joel can tell exactly where she is, about to break into joy, he wakes up and calls for his mother, cries out to her, and we plummet down into cool water. Once I wake in the morning and find him standing there beside the bed looking at us. We take him into bed. He doesn't talk about his father much but he misses him. I can tell the silences, or when he clears his throat and clears it again for long stretches as though he's about to cry but doesn't know it. And sometimes I live in a strange world where I am swimming underwater trying to rise to breathe, to keep my head out, trying to carry them, trying not to think or feel for Sarah. Sometimes we're all sad together as though the past is pulling us into pieces and I hold Maggie and Joel in a big bundle and we all hug together on the bed and hold eachother safe. We build our world together in the loft.

A weekend. Joel stays with her parents. We borrow their car and set off for the mountains together. Driving through the day with her sitting silently beside me. I can turn and look at her cool eyes with her serenity when she finds me there in my eyes, or when she doesn't a brittle nervousness on the brink of breaking into feeling into passion into pain, always just held on her side of the line. Nothing can be too bad if we have eachother. Toward night we find an old inn in a valley town. We sleep in a small room upstairs and make love and finally fall asleep to the sound of a train going by our window. But the town doesn't have any trains but we both hear the freight train rumbling rattling by our window into sleep. Maggie dreams about a train coming through her life with Joe at the head of it, Joe's body is the train, and the engine is his face and open mouth. The train comes roaring through our lives and brings Joe's death with it, and she is afraid it will crush our lives and tries to keep it out, but that is the train we went to sleep to barreling toward us, rattling past our window, a train from no-where, no one's train but ours, she says. We fall asleep again but I wake up suddenly. There's a knock on the door. We lie there without answering. Go see she says. I go to the door and open and there's a girl I've never seen before. She has blond hair and uneven teeth biting her lip. She says where is someone and she says the man's name but I don't know what she means. And she says isn't he here? And I say no I'm just here, we're in this room now. Her face takes surprise then turns like Sarah's when I left and she runs away down the stairs. I hear a car start up outside and drive off.

The place belongs to an old school friend. It was once his family's farm. Now there is a huge old house on the side of the hill, old fields and a forest. There is a caved-in house across the drive and barns. It is the last place on a dirt dead-end road, overlooking the whole reservoir below which filled the river bed and valley when they dammed it up but you can still see where the two rivers run into the reservoir upstream. I used to fish one of them when I was a kid just around the bend where the hill comes down to the water. The house has twenty empty rooms and Maggie and Joel and I live for a month upstairs in the bare master bedroom with a fireplace kept burning for it is not quite summer. We cook downstairs in the old kitchen. I write from a room in the middle of the house and one afternoon as dusk comes up from the lake I hear bare feet pattering up to the door so I go and open the door but there's no one, nothing there. I think Maggie might have come and gone for it was a woman's step but I find her and Joel in the kitchen making supper and she looks at me and says they haven't left the room, and there's no one in the house. At night we huddle together in front of the fire with the empty rooms and unused fields around us.

I find Joel lying stretched out amid the lilies of the valley out front shaded over by the maple trees. I know the expression on his face, lying there quiet.

I think of Sarah sometimes. I sit out under a maple tree at the side of the house and look down at the reservoir and the black water like a well in me. The whole valley is flooded with black water. The water is calm, and there's heavy lush greenery all around it. I can't look down at the lake without thinking of Sarah, and I cry. Joel discovers me there crying and sort of pats my head and sits down beside me and won't go away. So I stop crying and he leads me off and we play together.

Maggie wanders through the rooms distraught. She is drawing and painting. Her picture is blocks of buildings and tenements with a skeleton astride, riding the buildings with its death's-head over the whole world she lived in. There is a woman in a window. In perspective I can see she must have foreknown Joe's death long ago, when he first embraced drugs, or when he went into the hospital, starting to worry, being afraid of it, two years of the hospital, knowing, not allowing herself to know. She did not want him to go to Mexico. The doctors told him not to go to Mexico, and then she took the long last trip with him to the edge of death with him and feeling him start to slip beyond her, riding the slow train out, she riding the train until the end and then jumped free.

I am sitting in the loft, alone, thinking of Sarah again. I walk to the telephone and call her, dial fingerfuls of digits, make a thousand-mile connection and find her suddenly as if she is waiting for me and always will be. Well hello, she says, it's you. It is hard to know anyone too well. I can graph her voice on a pain scale, on a love scale. She is ironic with me, objectively gentle, an intellectual. Busy with her thesis, little time to think, some friends, and how am I? I am hurting. I want to hang up but she keeps thinking of things to say, news of Morley, she took the dog to the vet, someone wants to marry her, the door lock broke and she cried not knowing what to do, silly of her, she says. She is signing the papers.

The plane lifts, leaves, it is a weekend flight worn like a pattern into my heart where the airport is always deserted and a woman in a purple coat is always waiting for me outside the gate, where we drive the flat cold highway into town getting used to eachother again in the dark, talking, starting up old rhythms. There is no one outside the gate. I take a bus into the city. I walk through empty downtown streets with my little bag and suit jacket over my shoulder toward the red light flickering on top of the radio tower out our front door and keep finding the red light shut out by tall buildings, losing me, appearing again over a parking lot. Into the honky-strip district among low flat buildings where we bought paint, a mattress, coat hangers, with the new dog straining at the leash in her hands. I am humming an old hymn, and we will build again Jerusalem in England's bright and . . . Past the hotel we stayed in looking for the apartment. Past the newspaper stand and grocery store with the red light strong overhead, on the dog walk we always took together since the weekend was so short. I keep thinking of her taking this walk while I was away, thinking of her waiting for me. I turn down our street heavy with summer trees and the dog sniffing full bushes, now walking in her footsteps expecting to see her ahead running like a girl with the huge dog under the street lamps. The small house painted gray, the windows are dark in the ground-floor apartment. The door is locked. I have no keys, left inside on the mantelpiece when I left, when the taxi came and I shoved my last moments into a suitcase forgetting everything, and hugged her goodbye not knowing it was goodbye yet, not believing it ever could be, that girl I married at college, our hopes, the safe world we made, the Adam and Eve on the mantelpiece, the room waiting to be painted where I'd work when . . . I ring the bell. I rap on the window, the burlap curtains are drawn, she made them while I nailed crossbeams and planks on a platform for the mattress, with a table built in for wine or whiskey glasses, and stained it chestnut. The room was white, the burlap was green, the African bedspread was green. Over the bed we hung a red rug woven with a leopard. And on the mantelpiece by her parents' candlesticks was the carved Adam and Eve holding an orange we always put over the bed where we made love. Over against the wall I put the old table for her to study on and built shelves over it for her books and underneath lined up records and the Mozart she played her silver flute to in college. But the room is dark. The dog doesn't bark. The cellar window has boards over it and there is no way to get in. I want to talk to her. I keep calling from the hotel. It is the same hotel we stayed in together only a different room. My service bag sits in the middle of one bed.

I lie down on the other. I phone. It's early enough for her to be out on a date. I shower and dress. I go out to the strip district for some food. The last customer, I eat fried shrimp and listen to the band next door. I phone, and go into the bar and phone, and watch a girl take off her clothes. The lights go on. The bar is closing. I wonder. It is late now. I walk back to our apartment. I rap on the dark glass. It's too warm for the windows to be closed. The dog doesn't bark. I sit on the front steps and listen to the wind push through the trees. They make the red light wink up through the girders. I write her a note in the dark saying "Dear Sarah, your husband came to visit and wishes to say this is a dreary honky town for aloneness, after an evening honking. He wants you to know he loved you and is sorry things got so tough. He loves you some-times but he tries not to think about you. He wants to say you are strong and beautiful. And he asks his wife to forgive him for lost innocence, and thanks her—" but I can't go on like that so I sign it and slip it under the door.

Back in the loft Maggie has left for a communal farm in the country and there's a note saying she loves me and will always love me even if I don't make up my mind. I'm alone without her or Joel. I walk around the city and see people and wait for her to come home. Finally I send her a telegram asking her to come home.

When Maggie comes home she tells me how beautiful it is to live again. She tells how the dirt road winds up through the orchards with the scent of apples and wet dust, how rain sparkles on the leaves as sunlight comes back to the hill, and up top the house leans into the valley and all around it are green pastures and planted fields. At first she slept alone in the tall grass. Looking down into the valley with its smaller hills was like looking down at her own bare body at the waterfall, that was all she had left. She put Joel to sleep in the house with the other kids and lay out in the high grass with the sky wide overhead, and with nothing to hold her back she let herself float up into the clusters of stars. The grass was wet in the mornings. She went up to the house for oatmeal. She went into the fields to pick snow peas for the stand, filling one hand then the other with green pods until her basket was full. She took off her shirt and picked bare like the others in the rising sun, moving from one plant to another. Patrick stood short brown and naked between rows of corn. The other girls picked beside her. When the sun was up they put the baskets in the back of the truck and the men drove it down to the stand. At the end of the day they all went swimming at the waterfall and one boy wanted to be with her but he belonged to the tall blonde with large breasts who walked like an Amazon and all the women had such good bodies they made her breasts feel small. And others wanted to sleep with her but she didn't feel like making love. When she wasn't picking or swimming or walking in the woods, she worked in the kitchen or played with Joel, or talked with Patrick who she said was the priest. He led the chanting every night before supper and he taught her to say the chant when she was scared, alone, so she wouldn't look at the dark blue mountains but down the road into the valley. Patrick took her walking one night after supper, short and jaunty like Joe in the old days beside her, making her laugh, stroking her arm as they all did as if she were some child and belonged to them. She was happy when they touched her. And when Patrick kissed her she had to bend her knees but she slept alone down in the fields. And woke with the grass wet, and picked, and made friends with the other women over the stove and sink. And one day she left Joel with the other children and worked the stand for a day with Patrick alone, and that night she let him come down in the field with her, and sleep there. But in the morning everyone at breakfast smiled at her so she tried to tell them about me she says, but a girl asked then why isn't he with you. And she couldn't answer so they smiled or stroked her arm as she sat silent listening to music in the meeting room. And that night she took his hand and went down into the field and she let him take her calling out to all of them who took care of her. She says sleeping with him was not so different from picking snow peas and she didn't have to sleep with him again or not sleep with him. And the next night there was no reason to say no so she let him come down to her again but that night his body drove her suddenly into pleasure bringing her down from the stars and all the others, and she called for Joe but it wasn't Joe, Joe was dead, calling for me but I wasn't there and she hated me, calling for anyone because she didn't know who it was in that hard body locked into her and she began to cry wondering where everyone had gone, why I wasn't there she says, why no one was there to help her. And then she came home.

So she tells me taking me apart piece by piece. It didn't mean anything, she says, that's why I came home. I stare at the ceiling. You can do what you want with me, she says, but I love you. I'm afraid I'll be lost to Maggie and nameless faceless Patrick, like Joe, like every man I'm not, to some beauty I don't have. And I won't be. I say we'll go back up together.

We can't talk. We can't sleep together. We drive in silence up through the orchards to the farmhouse. People, children. I can't look at them. The house is falling down. There is a beautiful blond girl with stretch marks on her breasts, her blouse is buttoned part way, her eyes are cold gray. Maggie knows them all and they know eachother. They greet us. I play with the children. At supper Maggie sits across from me, across a mat filled with bowls of rice, vegetables, bread and Kool-Aid, serving out food as though she belongs here. They all talk and laugh. The girl next to me sits with her leg firm against mine feeding her baby. She holds my eyes calm and unscared. In the middle of dinner Patrick and another man walk in. He stands there in the doorway in a blue and red stocking cap, a ragged red beard. He goes over to Maggie and pinches her bright red cheek. She stands up and he hugs her. Her eyes are open at me over his shoulder and as though he feels it he turns around to me stand-ing there, and smiles and says good, good, and holds out his hand to me. I look in those eyes smiling up at me, hard self-possessed eyes, and look at his hand in the silence. I grab the mat of his hair and try to ram his head against the door jamb. Two other men jump me. I see the bowls spilling on the supper mat and legs. I keep striking out and connecting but there are too many bodies. They hold me. They don't hurt me. They put me out the door. I wander out into the middle of the field where the sky is too big for me. I sit in the blurring grass. The sun is down. When it is dark Maggie brings our sleeping bags and lies down in the grass beside me.

A man gives me a poem. He takes it out of his wallet and the paper is worn and about to tear along the fold lines. He says keep it. It's an old calendar from *The White Goddess* by Robert Graves:

> I am a stag: of seven tines,
> I am a flood: across a plain,
> I am a wind: on a deep lake,
> I am a tear: the sun lets fall,
> I am a hawk: above the cliff,
> I am a thorn: beneath the nail,
> I am a wonder: among flowers,
> I am a wizard: who but I
> Sets the cool head aflame with smoke?

I am a spear: that roars for blood,
I am a salmon: in a pool,
I am a lure: from paradise,
I am a hill: where poets walk,
I am a boar: ruthless and red,
I am a breaker: threatening doom,
I am a tide: that drags to death,
I am an infant: who but I
Peeps from the unhewn dolmen arch?

I am the womb: of every holt,
I am the blaze: on every hill,
I am the queen: of every hive,
I am the shield: for every head,
I am the tomb: of every hope.

Maggie is picking, up in the fields. Someone is crying in the meeting room. I go in. There is a young girl there crying alone. I rock her until she goes to sleep. I find some tools and fix the door I broke. Maggie sleeps beside me in the field, without touching.

The truck leaves us off at the vegetable stand. Maggie and I sell all day and at dark wait for the truck to pick us up. The vegetables have to be put away in a freezer near town. It's dark. Maggie leaves me with the cashbox and the produce and walks back to the farm. The cars pass. I'm not sure she will come back. I think she will join Patrick and leave me here. I lie down on the benches to breathe. I will find out. But if she doesn't come back I have nowhere to go. I don't know where I am, or who I am. Then the truck drives up with two men, and Maggie in a car behind.

She drives. The moon is out. Up through the orchards gray leaves flutter in my chest. We go past the house down into the valley. She stops where the path leads off into the woods, we get out and walk. Over a ravine the trees part and the sky lights a path down below on the water. Sounds of running falling water. I follow her down the embankment, around a large rock, and there the waters stream off the rocks in silver, making white froth in the pool. She takes off her clothes. I strip. Her body is long and pale as a run of water when she slides into the pool. I catch my breath at the cold. I can't touch bottom. We can't talk in the roaring. We swim to where the water comes down off the high rocks pummeling the pool. She puts her hands up on my shoulders and we go under the fall together. The water beats us down together, clinging, until we break apart and push off the rocks to the surface, warm air. Moonlight. She pulls herself out on the stone. I get out. We look at eachother. Her nipples are like blackberries.

Back in the meeting room we sit with the others, listening. In a way I've lost her so I'm not afraid of losing her anymore. She keeps smiling at me the way she did at the waterfall, daring me to love her.

THREE

Conventional Wisdoms and Lies

Leaking Faucets

In Victorian times it was possible to turn three or more faucets into stoppered basins at different points in the house, at the same rate as overflow drainage from each basin, so as you walked from room to room you were continually greeted by trickling water, as in garden pools. A. K. Sowles recommended floating rose petals or lilac blooms so that entering the bathroom was accompanied by the real flower smell and the tiny purple flowers in a cluster were sprinkled with dew against the white porcelain.

When water like life is metered, a leaky faucet may make the difference of a bath a week.

To stop a leaking faucet, loosen the only nut in sight on the appliance and try to lift the knob and metal spike free. Hit it. Try again. Scoop out the remnants of the black washer from the hole with your little finger. Find a replacement at the hardware store and replace.

Myrna Robb recommends a cork. Sandra Russell suggests turning the water on and off at the tap beneath the basin instead. My former wife would ignore it. And a girl who called herself Wonder Forest, a corny but friendly hippie from Queens, New York, says, "Why don't you just let the sink fill up and float flowers in it?"

Another Plumbing Problem

There may come a time when the water rises, bearing the weight of what you wish to forget to the surface and over onto your tan leather shoes, the bath mat, or floor where your children play.

The water may subside and all that you need is a plunger, the kind boys joust with at camp, perched on the gunwales of canoes.

But the water may overflow again and seep out of the tub drain as well. The sink will not drain and the dishwater scatters its pool of suds on the kitchen floor around the cat's saucer. All this is likely to happen at once. It isn't altogether bad. It means finally you have to deal with a basic plumbing problem.

A. Locate the problem. Your septic tank often lies under a concrete circle with a ring in it children stub their toes on. Lift the ring in good spirits so the darkness below doesn't draw you into memories of the pain you have caused others. If the tank is full it must be pumped out. Call and a honey wagon will come. A true servant of society will draw up the contents of the septic tank into his honey wagon. Then it becomes his problem. Occasionally you will meet a person who acts as a honey wagon for the rest of us.

When the tank is dry you may pay the man extra to clean it, and he will descend on a sturdy ladder and scrape the insides. I have seen men so inured to their job that they will take their lunch passed down through the manhole, sitting on a ladder rung. Such men have a wry and subversive sense of humor.

If the water rises a third time over and onto your floor, and if the new wastage does not pour out into the tank and down the boots of the poor man you have forgotten there eating his sandwich, a clogging exists somewhere in the network of pipes through or under your house.

If you must pretend you have only a minor problem

feed a small metal snake down through the bowl. The snake will stop fairly soon at a right-angle turn in your piping.

Move to the basement. Locate the main pipe which collects the drains from above before it plunges down under the earth. The joint will not undo easily, it is packed with lead or cement and you may have to break this with a stone chisel. Remember when you break into the main pipe the accumulation from the fixtures above will empty directly from the hole you have made. Try inserting a large snake here, first in one direction then the other, as far as it will go. You can also insert the snake through the pipe that empties into your tank. In the worst of all possible worlds the clogging will lie out of reach, well protected by articulate bends in the pipe, impacted and petrified with slow accumulation and neglect, fortified with articles you thought you had thrown from your life forever, congealed into a rather impressive sculpture of our modern life. You may just have to dig at some point where you think the pipe will be. And if you hit it, chisel a hole through its upper surface and with the bilge rising around you insert once more the metal tape.

By now there is a real joy when the snake meets its obstruction and begins to bite through it, when you realize once again that you will admit no impediment to a clean and wholesome life, when with a rush and gurgle the wastage in the pit around you begins to subside and your fresh pack of cigarettes floats like Odysseus' bark into Charybdis, then run outside into the clean air and morning sun—it is the blue sky of early summer, and watch down in the septic tank the sudden gushing forth and release, as in Scotland after a rain the waterfalls and flumes pour from the sides of green hills bouncing their arcs or rainbows to meet the new sun. And notice how others standing around you, drawn by the mechanics of release, will point and say "What do you suppose that is? Or that?" examining, poking and prying amid the crap of life, repelled and fascinated by the surface of its changing forms, while you who have immersed yourself, can try to speak of waterfalls and rainbows and begin to make the world again, new and beautiful.

Horrors of This World: A Partial Listing

Leaking Faucets
Septic Tanks
Catheterization
Literary Figures
Divorce
Betrayal

Rich Girls
Sharks while Swimming
Mothers with Scissors
Naked Fathers
War
Heroin Addiction
Lost Love
Forget-me-nots
Hateful Parents
Spoiled Children
Boredom
Lynching
Portions of Our History
Mad Dogs
Self-righteousness
Death of a Parent
Death of a Lover
Death of a Child
Death of a Rich Elderly Person
Death of a Hope
Non-specific Urethritis
Military Officers
Someone with Someone You Love
When Your Wife Has a Baby by Another Man
Growing Old
Impotence
Frigidity
Lack of Money
Too Much
Failure
Worldly Success
Sickness Unto Death

A Boss Who Is an Idiot
Your Own Sharkiness
Cancer
Your Own Imminent Death
False Professors
Shatteredness
Fear
Lack of Feeling
Perfection
Frame-ups
Atomic Explosions
Wastage
The Yellow Peril
The Black Peril
The Red Peril
The White Peril
Selfishness
Devils
Blackmail
An Angry God

On dealing with the horrors of this world: I talk
about them and try to work them into the beauty of
awareness. It is better not to ignore them, but make
them less horrible by work, sweat and blood, write
them out like the few stories that we made end well,
and give the wisdom to eachother.

Sharks

There is nothing innately frightening about sharks unless you are in the water with one.

A BATTLE WITH THE HORROR OF LIFE

On December 20, 1966, Mr. and Mrs. Frank Boyd and Mr. and Mrs. James Wilson went swimming at the ocean beach near Sarasota, Florida. It was 11:35 p.m. There was a three-quarter moon. Mr. Wilson describes what happened as follows:

Frank and Nora and I were treading water talking about the party, Bea had drifted off a little way. She was shy and hadn't wanted to come in. I heard her gasp and turned around to see her surface in a pool of phosphorescence. Nora said we should go to shore. I swam to Bea but she kept slipping out of my arms, yanked underwater by something bigger than both of us. She would come up again whining, thrashing, until I grabbed her arm and started to pull her toward shore. Something brushed my leg and the salt water stung. The only other thing I remember was the peculiar taste in the water. I carried her out on the beach and gave her mouth-to-mouth resuscitation. The flesh was stripped from her leg. Frank ran up to the house to call an ambulance and find us all something to put on. Later a marine biologist came by the hospital and said it was a tiger shark, he could tell by the positioning of the teeth marks.

Whale and basking shark are thirty or forty feet long and eat plankton. The others will eat almost anything but they have different-sized mouths. There are makos, mackerels, man-eaters, tigers, bulls, lemons, duskies, nurses, and others.

Each type of shark has its peculiarities of shape and size and behavioral patterns. The positive identification of a shark is best made after a close inspection of the teeth. The man-eater's teeth, for example, have serrated edges, the mako has a little cusp near the base of the denture and the porbeagle none, just its row of canines. The shark's teeth are so sharp that men bitten say they did not feel the first bite. The size of a shark bite depends on the size of the shark's mouth.

Biologically, sharks are something between a fish and a mammal. Young sharks are born alive and immediately start functioning like miniature reproductions of their parents. The mother offers no food or protection and if hungry may eat her young.

Anatomically, a shark has no swim bladder. This flotation device allows other fish to remain motionless in any space of water, but the shark must keep swimming or he will sink. So from birth until death he swims, dozing as he moves through protective waters, a fugitive from his own death.

Sharks are unpredictable. You can drag bait within inches of a shark's nose and he may ignore it. But if there is a slight trickle of blood from the bait the shark will attack senselessly. On the open sea you can watch a shark intersect a blood trail. He can follow the trail to its inception, turn a hundred and eighty degrees and come back the other way, or he may come directly to your bait.

Torpedoed, men sat in the water waiting for rescue while sharks ate them at leisure. In open seas it is suggested that you form groups with others in your own position, preferably excluding wounded or bleeding men, in hopes that the shark will think you a larger animal than he. Men in such clusters have beat the water with their arms and legs and scared sharks off. Others have beat the water with their arms and legs and have been eaten. Once a man scared a shark by hitting him on the nose with an underwater camera. You can try to poke out the shark's eyes or dig your nails into his throat but there is no reason to think this will do any good. You can pray.

According to a booklet issued PT-boat personnel, a man who finds himself in the water with a shark grabs the shark by the dorsal fin and rams a knife up under into the shark's stomach, drawing it backward to eviscerate. Now it is true that if you can slit a shark's stomach from end to end its guts will fall out. But a blue shark has been observed calmly eating its own entrails. Shark hides were used by skilled craftsmen before sandpaper, and it is extremely hard to slit a shark's stomach even in a fish factory. In the water, as soon as the shark feels a knife tickle his stomach he takes off like a shot to return from a different angle. It is better not to try to kill a shark when you are both in the water. The scent of blood, including his own, seems to increase his anger. It is better to have nothing to do with him (*fn*. Shark Repellent: like a gas mask, something neither you nor I is likely to have if we need).

There are deep-sea fishermen who cut bait if they get a shark on the line. Others deal with shark in the following manner: bring the shark alongside, slip a knife into its gills and slice outward so the shark eventually bleeds to death. (This method may attract other sharks, a multiplication of sins.) Or, slip a rope around the shark's tail and hoist him aloft so the stomach presses down on the shark's brain and frequently out of his mouth. (This may result in considerable damage to boat and onlookers since it is dangerous to lift anything that large by the tail.) Or, put a good hook in the shark's mouth and hoist him aloft, strapping him around the middle to the mast. Even out of water it may take a shark six or seven hours to die. Man-eaters last longest. Some people shoot shark but it is an uncertain sport furthered by those who have lost parts of themselves or close relatives to the sharks of this world. A hit in the brain is the only sure kill, and the brain is exceedingly small, shaped rather like a wishbone. A three-inch naval gun will do the job if a direct hit is scored. One can wrap a hand grenade in beef with the fishline attached to the pull pin. But then the shark may swim toward you.

The truth of the matter is that, except for the occasional shark landed on a fishing boat or jostled by a depth charge, sharks are practically indestructible. Always moving, always hunting, like evil they assure the randomness and uncontrollability of life itself.

Afterthoughts: much of our horror of sharks comes from no shark at all but a dying cod flashed out of some fisherman's net. We fear the shark in ourselves, having gutted a friend, or slashed the innocence of young love, torn apart some opponent, or bite by bite teased our parents into skeletons. It is the quick gunmetal turn and darting of our own minds that rises up toward us in those night waters and threatens to discover our blood.

Wonder Forest says that most people in power are sharks. They play amid a school of dolphins.

A sand road runs outside my house back into the dunes and footprints are soon blown over. There are primrose on either side, blueberry bushes, and on the field in back of the house there is a fishnet fishermen left to dry years ago. Now the grass and blueberry bushes grow up through it, Queen Anne's lace, little snowflowers. A few buttercups lie amid the long grass.

I don't pick them. They shine up from the green like bits of the sun. And the earth keeps pushing up her free treasure.

Rich Girls

It is quite possible that rich girls are not among the horrors of this world at all, and my own susceptibility came from a lack of money. This section then is recommended to young men who have only the hard currency of their own bodies and looking at a rich woman are tempted to get Something for Nothing.

Often it is difficult to distinguish a rich girl from any other girl. Nowadays she may masquerade as a secretary or computer programmer. If her mother went into hospital visiting committees or benefits, she may find her way into foundations or Republican politics. Frequently the only way of spotting a rich girl is by the company she keeps. The boss will take a special interest in her. She may well direct her energies to pleasing some older man, possibly her father. Life will be essentially a game. If a girl over a period of time seeks total moral or sexual obliteration and continually manages to survive it, she may be or may plan to be a rich girl. Rich girls often shut horror out of their lives, but then someone else may have to pick up the tab. Intelligent rich girls tremble continually on the brink of this realization. Nothing is ever quite a rich girl's fault. She is merely water finding her own course through gaiety or catastrophe exhibiting the same slightly numbed coolness. She is an actress in a world of real people.

The rich girl achieved a mythic stature in the late fifties, as shown in this anonymous poem of the time:

The Poet to His Love

You are a land of milk and honey,
You are a desert filled with rain,
Your banks are filled with money,
Your fields with waving grain,
Your clouds have a silver lining,
Your streets are paved with gold,
Your whole is good for mining,
Your luck will always hold,
Your cup is running over,
Your well spouts precious oils,
Your market value's growing,
Since I have found your spoils.
Your lips are red like rubies,
Your scent like new-minted bills,
And the very set of your boobies
Cries "Gold in them thar hills."
Your hips are heaps of uranium,
Yet soft as a bed of clover,
I think a pink geranium
Blooms when you bend over.
Teeth of pearl! Diamond eyes!

My goddess! My salvation!
You have made my good stock rise
Happy with inflation.
For nowhere is there greater treasure,
Not even in Fort Knox,
Than all those riches of earthly pleasure
I found in your strongbox.

I was myself once a poor and unsuccessful poet, which may have been one reason I was drawn to my own rich girl. She had generous breasts, ill hidden in a wool suit, and eyes like blue ice. She had a strong intelligent mind and was then secretary to the head of a large foundation. She awkwardly performed her exercises every night before she went to bed. She ate a great deal of cottage cheese. When I took her flowers she put them in a white vase and made them last. She was warm, loving, and exceedingly generous.

She did suggest that it was not entirely necessary to be poor and struggling. She introduced me to wealthy friends, in particular the head of that foundation which gave large grants to young poets. He was delighted. She told me to apply for a grant. I did and received a substantial sum of money. We had spent most of it when a mutual friend told me my rich girl was once the foundation head's mistress, though the man was over fifty with a wife and three grown children. He was also overweight and spittle accumulated when he talked at the corners of his mouth which he touched from time to time with a blue polka-dotted handkerchief. But she assured me there had been nothing for years, and what had been was essentially the old man's fantasy since he had not been able et cetera. I was happy to believe. My increased understanding of the man allowed me tolerance and occasionally he came to pleasant dinners where he brought wines of esoteric vintage and flattered my work. Though I can remember times too when he put his hand on my girl's shoulder or knee an instant too long: she assured me that was his manner in giving advice, and laughed at my petty jealousies, a wellspring of my youth.

And I suppose I would still not find rich girls horrifying at all if it were not for a curious set of circumstances and coincidences.

When my grant was spent, and in the back of my mind I was thinking how to survive the year ahead (I began identifying with office clerks again), her boss invited us to spend a weekend with his family in Darien, Connecticut.

They lived in an old stone farmhouse where the main field was mowed into lawn. The big red barn was a guesthouse with white trim and a freshly painted Pennsylvania Dutch hex sign. The children were not there. He greeted us warmly, mentioned a renewal of my grant, and introduced me to his wife, a younger gray-haired woman with a graciously full body kept in bounds by her flower-print dress.

She took my arm as we walked through their gardens, her hand was soft with clear lacquered nails. She told me the names of flowers as we walked, when they bloomed, and how she and her husband waited patiently for each. We joined her husband and my girl back at the house. The dinner was elegant, the wine abundant between us. Talk turned toward politics where they proved to be secret revolutionaries but we had to promise not to tell. After a while the foundation head took my rich girl off to see the work of some applicants, indeed he had to decide very soon who would receive the monies, while his wife sat in a white armchair across from me, smiling, running her fingers lightly over the fabric. She poured another brandy. She touched her hair. She brought the glass toward me and leaned over to hand it to me revealing her tanned breasts to the nipples. I got to my feet, wanting her but then not wanting myself. I mumbled an excuse and went to the bathroom where I cupped fresh water in my hands and splashed it on my face. I thought I heard someone calling me through the other door to the bathroom. The sound continued. I dried my face and hands and opened the door and there was the foundation head in the leather chair of his study with his legs apart where my rich girl knelt in a ceremony of devotion.

She wrote me a letter once, later, saying that she loved me, saying there were a great many things I did not understand, that she did what she was doing for us, but she knew I would not believe that. And in fact I cannot accept it because that is where the horror comes from, the part of me that believes her, and loves her, and wanted her to.

Mad Dogs

One of the rules of my town was that dogs couldn't run free. Caught dogs were ransomed at a twenty-five-dollar fee, which was what it cost to get your car back if you parked in front of the firehouse door. I kept him chained to an iron stake in the back yard.

I used to let him roam free a good deal, figuring I would not pay the ransom and he could live with the other dogs in the town kennel. But I found that dogs unclaimed at the kennel were taken to the state veterinary offices and put to sleep.

I'm not about to have the neighbors say, "He let his own dog be gassed by the state," which is why I kept him chained to the stake in my back yard. When he was chained securely it was very hard for him to be a bad dog. It was when I let him off the chain that the trouble began, and so I learned how to deal with a bad dog.

HOW TO DEAL WITH A BAD DOG

Some people say dogs are bad because they have been poorly trained. Perhaps the dog's mother left him when he was too young, perhaps the dog's father used to playfully bite through his son's floppy ears. I do not know about this. I thought if a dog was bad he was an annoyance, and would stop most directly if I hit him. I learned this was a mistake.

With my own dog the game played out in the following manner. There were some mornings when I woke stunned perhaps by the fullness of a summer day or the early song of birds, and instead of tying my dog to his stake in the back yard, I fed him by the kitchen door, unfettered, and then tied him. On occasion, I embarked on some small project before leaving for work and opened the door on two empty feed bowls and no dog at all. I called him. I whistled. I called him nicely and said "Good doggie, come, come, Rufus." And nothing happened. So I set out to find my dog and save him.

Sometimes he was hiding in a little grove of scrub oak over the hill. Sometimes he was playing at the water's edge down by the pond, rolling in the mud, or splashing out amid the lily pads. Sometimes he was pawing through an overturned garbage can looking for snacks. Or nosing the bulldog who guarded the trailer park. Sometimes he was playing with the children who lived down the street, cavorting among them, leaping with all four feet off the ground and dashing in and out amid their wagons. He was very playful and though large, they knew he didn't bite and became fond of him. It made me very angry because I was out hunting for him and worrying, worrying, while he was having such a good time. I took him away. When we got to the shielded place on the dirt road I hit him up alongside the mouth and swore at him. Once a group of children came upon us, and one of them yelled "Mad dog!" and they all ran away. It was the children who saved us.

Parents

"It's not that simple. Of course you hate your parents. No, of course you do. But you also love them a great deal, that's why you're thinking about them at all, you love them and you just don't know how to accept that. You are self-pitying, you a person of some intellect, sliding around, wasting your time. Let me tell you two stories. This is the first. Now I've always hated my mother, I have since I was a child. She was always getting married and she had no time for me. She was a very beautiful woman, she looks a little like me when I'm thin but her bone structure is much finer. She resented me, especially when I became a young woman, and she never did a thing beyond what was expected of her. That's how I felt about the matter.

"Well, I was seven months pregnant and in the hospital in Hartford, which I don't want to talk about, when the state police called and told me my stepfather, that's my mother's third husband, had an accident on the Massachusetts Turnpike and was dead. My mother who was in the car was seriously injured in the hospital so I got out of bed and went to her.

"It turned out Mother had a brain injury and was unconscious. The hospital was not sufficient so I moved her to a hospital in Boston, and rode with her there in the back of a converted Cadillac holding the plasma bottle. She was unconscious and the whole time I sat there all I could think was Mother please wake up, please wake up, because I wanted to tell her I loved her. I had never told her really that I loved her and I didn't want her to die without knowing that.

"She was still unconscious the next day. My brother came down, stunned and bumbling, and the doctor told us he was going to have to operate. I know something about brain operations, having gone through several of them with an older friend, so when we were alone I asked the doctor and he said Mother had only about twenty percent chance of surviving the operation at all. No, I didn't tell my brother. We went up to her room before the operation. I went in first and Mother lay there with her hair all shaved and the wound in her head and I turned right around and took my brother by the arm and led him out for a cup of coffee. I didn't want him to see her like that for the last time. They took her down to the operating room and we had to leave and go bury my stepfather.

"Mother did survive the operation and I got to tell her I loved her. Of course she didn't change a bit. When I got divorced she sided with my husband, and the last time I was in New York I went to see her for twenty minutes. 'Twenty minutes, Sarah, is that all the time you want to spend with your own mother?' 'Yes, it is, Mother, it's all I can stand, but you know I love you, don't you.' And she does."

The Death of Your Own Parents

When I was younger I could not have survived my parents' death. I remember as a boy I lived for them, when they ate dinner at home the world was full and joyful. I would lie awake nights waiting for them to come home from a party. My young life was bursts of warmth between summer camp and boarding school. I never saw enough of my parents. Having taken the bait hook and all, they let me run far behind the boat, swimming as fast as I could through heavy seas, always trying to catch up with their joy, to be one with them, to be out of the water and in the boat. I grew, and swam faster, more strongly, but their boat was ahead of me, bobbing on the waves with its little yellow canopy puffing in the wind. Sometimes I could hear the voices of their friends on the breeze, "He's a good one, how fast and strong he is, look how his colors are iridescent when he jumps in the sun." And my parents might nod and smile. One day I realized I would never catch up with their love. The bait they threw to the waters gave no nourishment. I hoped they loved me but knew they might not see me as I am. Their love also masked a deeper search of their own. Maybe it's by compassion you understand these things. The jealousy of a mother for her daughter. A father's fear of his son. And good things. The lessons are not shocking, it is love that brings these feelings together. Not the love to build a world with perhaps, but stronger than the anguished cry of humanity as the hearth grows cold. Forgive. The little boat is somewhere out on the wide troughs of the waves and in our own lives we are kinder than sharks, you and I.

When Your Wife Has a Baby by Another Man

This sort of problem does not occur casually. It takes a great deal of effort on the part of at least three people—one of those intricate structurings of possible realities which occurs down through history again and again, is suffered and survived with struggle of soul which finally yields a private peace.

My own thoughts on the matter are that it is not horrible at all unless you make it so. And if your wife has a baby by another man it is probably your own fault.

My good friend Will was a man who sought torment with a moral fervor. Wellborn and the product of a protected childhood, he walked open-eyed into the various hells available to him, thinking this might put him more in touch with the rest of mankind, and reveal several of the secrets of life. To sustain his endeavors he married Sarah, a full-bodied graduate student who could both respect such nonsense and yet realize it had nothing to do with her. She was in school looking for a husband. I remember her walking down the sidewalks of Cambridge smiling, with heavy volumes clasped to her belly like the weight of a child.

Impervious to his gloom, she was swayed by love made in desperation and the curative power of her own resilient vitality, and went to live with Will, who, after many ups and downs in attempt to instill some sense of tragedy in this buoyant young lady, gave up and married her. They were reasonably happy. He began to feel he had betrayed the journey of his life and was fast losing interest in the miseries of the world, which began to hurt his work as a radical politician. He saw himself as a fat bourgeois, a betrayer of Misery, an eater of steak and drinker of wine with a charge card at his wife's breast. Sarah saw her husband less of a youth and more of a man, ready to give her the children she wanted and finally raise a family. Now I have never fully understood why he did not give Sarah children, I doubt he understands it himself. It may be something as simple as his refusal to burden the world with any continuation of himself. Or it may have had a good deal to do with Sarah. She finally said to him, "Sweetheart, you promised me a baby this year." He said, "We don't have a cent in the bank." She said, "If we wait too long I'll be too old to have children." Whereupon he went out and fell in love with a ballet dancer.

Poor Sarah was crushed, for about eight months. But whereas Will drifted on downward to a confronta-

tion with his own misery, Sarah with her usual resil-
iency found a nice clean-cut biochemist and promptly
found they could make a baby quite easily, putting to
rest fears instilled long ago by her mother, and doub-
ling her radiance and vitality. When Will, battered
and torn beyond his own recognition and so accus-
tomed to misery that the very word "unfortunate" filled
him with a vague apathetic dread, found her out again,
in the same suit he left in with hair unwashed over
his collar, and his eyes filled with a rare hope glistening under his brow, he stood on the doorstep of the
marvelously structured house she now lived in with
the biochemist, and she opened the door pale, quite
beautiful, and seven months pregnant, with her hair
in a soft wreath above her sleepy smile. And in that
instant he realized that another man had given her life
where he had failed to: it is the kind of recognition
that is fleeting, one carries it around close to one's
waking life at the risk of severe debilitation, and he
was faced with the problem at the center of his own
misery.

She was of course very sweet, and asked him in for
a cup of coffee, and said she didn't necessarily want a
divorce, that was all up to him, that she was quite
happy having a child, and the biochemist was sweet
to her so that she found life bountiful and was sorry

he did not find his lot at the moment quite so joyful.

How Will handled the problem: he couldn't. He muttered a few words about how he hoped she would be happy and stumbled out the door to weep. This amused no one. On the way back to his hotel he walked into the side of a moving car which spun him into a lamppost. He drank half a bottle of whiskey and fell asleep.

It was hard to follow his course through the following months. I would see him at the movies with one girl, waiting outside the drugstore for another. In a drunken moment he confided he was trying to sleep with all his wife's friends. I don't know what he was doing for money. Rumor said he was about to marry an heiress. I didn't ask him. He looked lean, his eyes glittered, a bright red tie spilled down his chest. Then he dropped out of sight completely.

One Sunday afternoon several years later he appeared on my doorstep with a pale lovely girl who was evidently about to have a baby. He introduced his new wife. They were living in Chicago where he worked for her uncle's company. They planned to have lots of children. The girl smiled and took his hand. He said by the way what ever happened to Sarah? I told him the biochemist had reconciled with his wife, and she and the little boy were living with her parents. He said oh and looked out the window as if letters of blood were written up in the sky. But when I looked there was nothing, just a sunny blue factual day.

Death of a Lover

If you love with your heart and soul this death wounds your marriage to life. Ordering your life into wisdoms does not justify the pain. Stupid little wisdoms are no help. Faith turns bitter. Utter despair is too self-concerned. It seems there is no containment. If you suffer this you may pay hardest if you try to deal with it at all. It seems I'm often wrong. But it may be best to accept the madness and live it out. If you live with religion go to your men of god and give your life up to them until you are well. If you cannot abide religion give your life up to helping others until you are healed. And if you cannot stand to look on any face which does not understand that what you loved more than all the world has died, withdraw into the wilderness for a while or throw yourself into the sea of humanity around you until everyone else's pain tempers your own.

Shatteredness

Each fragment said to me do this no do this and I didn't know which one to listen to. So I went to men of god and said I don't know anything. I don't know what to do. Help me. And they took me in.

A brother was plowing a field and he gave me shears to cut off the dead branches that hung out over the field and got in the way of the tractor. And cut off the live branches around the field so the tractor could pass easily and their shade wouldn't stunt the growth of the grain. So I cut off the dead branches and it terrified me. And I cut the budding live branches and I kept wanting to leave the long sweeping ones, so they would flower, but the brother said no, cut all the branches out over the field so the tractor can pass and the grain can grow. And I saw I was afraid to cut the branches because I was afraid I was like the deadwood or the single branch budding alone.

A brother was plowing the field and he called for me to come over and showed me a whippoorwill with a spotted back and two-inch bill lying in the grass, while the tractor stalled and sputtered over it. Then I saw a little speckled bird at the edge of the furrow and I turned it over but the head was gone and the stomach rolled down into the furrow like a clod of earth. And the mother picked up and flew away. And the tractor moved on.

The brothers had plowed a small garden near the chaplain's house. And they gave me storm fences to circle the freshly turned earth. So I put in the stakes and buried the fence two feet deep so the ground hogs wouldn't burrow under but I kept seeing that I wasn't building a fence around a garden but a patch of fresh earth. I was fencing in raw earth, so that one day it might be a garden.